# LYCAN WITCH

## SILVER WOLVES OF LOCKWOOD

### BOOK TWO

WHITNEY MORSILLO

If you purchased this book without a cover, you should be aware that this book is stolen property. It was reported as "unsold and destroyed," and the author has not received any payment for this "stripped book."

This book is a work of fiction. The names, characters, businesses, places, events, locales, and incidents are the products of the author's imagination or have been used fictitiously and are not to be construed as real. Any resemblance to actual persons, living or dead, actual events, locales or organizations is entirely coincidental.

ISBN 9798861100397

Copyright © 2023 by Whitney Morsillo.

All rights reserved. Published independently by Whitney Morsillo, and any associated logos are trademarks and/or registered trademarks of Whitney Morsillo.

*To the witches and the she-wolves who love a morally gray man—may this spice be the perfect pay-off for that slow burn between your thighs*

*She was his light;*
*He was her darkness.*
*The stars whispered among them,*
*The troubles,*
*The rumors,*
*The pain.*
*But none knew that his darkness caressed hers at night.*
*None knew that her light lit him up from inside,*
*That he wrapped her so tightly in his arms*
*The arrows never pierced her,*
*Or that she didn't smooth his jagged edges*
*But fit her own tight against them.*
*The only thing that was spoken,*
*The truth no one dared question,*
*Was that to lay a finger on one*
*Meant to seek the wrath of the other.*
*For the others who had touched her*
*Had their screams added to the chorus of Tartarus,*
*I didn't know, I didn't know,*
*I didn't know.*
*But they did.*
*They just wished he didn't.*

# CHAPTER ONE
## *Adara*

SUNLIGHT PEEKS THROUGH THE BLINDS AS IT crests high above the trees, painting the backs of my eyelids golden. I roll over groggily and sigh, the scent of cedarwood and smoke filling my nose. My mouth goes dry as reality teases the edges of my mind before crashing into me.

I swallow hard, remembering last night—remembering *him*—and open my eyes. The morning light bathes the bedroom in a warm glow. The large oak bed is covered in white sheets with a thick pale green blanket tangled around my legs. The walls are painted a light mint with a dark mahogany door across from me and matching wood accents scattered throughout the space—a nightstand table between the bed and the window, the dark oak framing around the glass, and a dresser across the room from the bed.

It all feels so... light. So warm. So welcoming. So... not what I pictured for Gideon's house.

Gideon's house.

I roll onto my back and stare at the ceiling as I let that thought sink in.

I'm in Gideon Disantollo's house.

The faint smell of bacon greets my nose, and my stomach rumbles loudly in response. I can't remember the last time I ate, having had only enough energy to shower off the ashes and grime once I got here last night.

Gideon's eyes flash in my mind, the way they seemed to blaze when he saw me come out of the bathroom in just a towel, my damp hair hanging over my shoulders and dripping onto the floor. *"I... don't have anything to wear."* Glancing down, I look at the white t-shirt he loaned me—*his* t-shirt—and try to wipe the smile off my face.

I'm not here because of him. I'm here because Monique tried to *kill me*. Because she threatened to kill Jules. Because I had nowhere else to go and I had to walk into the literal wolf's den.

I rub my hand over my face and groan, rolling over to bury my face in the pillow. My stomach growls again, and I finally cave and drag myself out of bed. Tiptoeing down the hall, I slowly step downstairs and listen for voices.

Is Gideon here?

The thought of him cooking breakfast for me makes my heart beat faster, but the sound of a woman humming drifts up the stairs, jealousy sharply tugging in my chest. I stumble down a few steps, my wolf enraged that he would have another woman here when I'm sleeping in his bed.

*He's mine.*

Pausing on the landing, I shake my head. He isn't mine. He's a wolf, the most dangerous wolf in existence.

*And our mate,* my wolf reminds me.

With a huff, I ignore her, still uneasy that she can speak to me like this. I quietly walk into the kitchen, relief flooding my veins as I see Mila dancing along to the radio, humming the lyrics of a pop song as she flips bacon in a fry pan.

She glances over at me and smiles. "Addy! You're awake. See? I told you she'd be down soon." She throws a glance over her shoulder with a wink, and my eyes follow her gaze to the open kitchen window.

"Kaylus?" I ask, tears pooling in my eyes. "Is everything okay? Is Jules—"

He caws, flying to land on my shoulder, nuzzling his beak into my cheek. *"She's fine. She's with Chloe. They're hiding in one of the coven apartments... Are you okay?"*

I look into his black beady eyes, grateful to have at least one reliable friend in my life, and nod my head. "I'm okay. I..." I glance at Mila, who's back to dancing and humming. *"I used magic last night,"* I tell him silently.

*"Magic... like a spell?"*

*"No, magic like fire. Fire, Kaylus. I... burned the house down."* My lips flatten, realizing the home I grew up in and everything in it is gone in the wake of my flames. I look down at my hands, examining my palms

but seeing nothing there. No smoke, no flames, and no idea how to call upon it again.

Kaylus ruffles his feathers, snapping my attention back to the room before me.

The kitchen is the opposite of the bedroom I slept in. Black cabinets line the walls with stainless steel appliances scattered throughout. A black marble countertop with silver accents swirling through it to match the light gray backsplash enhances the feel of the room. It would feel cold in here—masculine and distant—if not for the warm wood floors and the large window taking up most of the farthest wall, which frames a view of the forest. Bright leaves are scattered along the ground below the bare branches that stretch up into the sky.

"Gideon had a meeting, but he should be back soon." Mila sneaks a glance at me before plating the rest of the food.

"I didn't..." I know I didn't ask, but I can't deny the slight disappointment that nags me, knowing he isn't here.

She shrugs. "I just thought you might want to know why it was me cooking breakfast in his house. He didn't want you to wake up alone."

I chew on my lower lip, glancing at Kaylus still sitting on my shoulder. Why does that make me feel so... happy? Why did he care to make sure I wasn't here alone? So I wouldn't run away and spill his secrets? Or so the coven couldn't capture me and force me to give away his pack knowledge?

*You know why,* my wolf says, bringing up the memory of Gideon's face when I banged on the bar door last night.

*The scent of rain surrounded me, Gideon's eyes devouring me before he pulled me inside. His lips, soft at first, then unyielding, demanding, until he pulled away suddenly. The sound of his claws carving into the door on either side of my head made goosebumps flare along my skin.*

*"What happened?" he asked, his voice deep and menacing, the promise of revenge dancing in his silver eyes. "Please don't make me ask again,* mia fiamma.*"*

*That name, that godsforsaken name. I never cared to know what it meant. I figured it was something degrading, something rude. Like* little witch. *But this time, in that moment, it took every ounce of self-control to not ask him, every ounce of strength to not latch myself onto him and beg him to forget me. Because Monique will kill him the second she gets the chance.*

*"You're not alone, little witch." With one sentence, he tore down the rest of my defenses, and I crumbled. "I'm the villain, and I'll burn the whole world down, sacrifice every innocent life in this world, just to save your soul."*

How could he say that? How could he promise something so big—so powerful and full of love—to his sworn enemy? To a witch. To *me*.

But he did.

The questions burn on my tongue, and the frustration that he isn't here to answer them makes my skin itch.

"Addy?" Concern etches across Mila's face, her hands full of plates covered with scrambled eggs and bacon. "Your eyes..."

I shake my head, clearing my mind and blinking away the wolf I know is trying to claw her way to the surface, desperate to reach her mate. I smile at Mila, embarrassed.

"You'll get used to her," she says, bumping my shoulder gently with hers as she moves to sit down at the breakfast bar. "It took me a good two months to get used to hearing mine in my head, let alone get comfortable shifting and trying to control that." She laughs at the memory with a shake of her head.

I try to brush it off as Kaylus flies to the counter, pecking at some seeds Mila left out for him, and I move to sit on the stool beside her. The large window in front of us gives a beautiful view of the fog strewn forest, the scent of wet bark and morning dew wafting inside.

"Plus, I hear after meeting your mate it becomes even harder to control it."

My eyes snap over to her as she stares down at her plate, a blush fiercely climbing across her cheeks while she pushes her eggs around.

She lifts one shoulder slightly, one corner of her mouth raising to reveal a small dimple. "Not that Gideon told me anything. It's just... obvious."

"Obvious?" I whisper, barely able to get the word out around the lump in my throat. If it's that obvious, does Monique know? Has she told the coven? A bonded wolf has never been tested for the immortality essence... and an alpha's mate bond is the strongest known. It would be impossible to talk them out of hunting me if they knew.

Mila's eyes snap to mine, and I'm struck by how pretty she is—her eyes are such a light blue they remind me of ice on a winter morning. She's curvy in all the places that I'm not, and the dimples in her cheeks, framed by warm blonde strands, offer a sense of innocence.

*But Gideon never spares her a passing glance.*

My wolf's words ring in my mind, sending sparks of bliss through me before I shove it all away. I can't claim him as mine. It's a death sentence for the both of us, and... and he's Gideon Disantollo, the man who almost killed one of his pack in front of me.

My wolf scoffs, irritated that I refuse to see that situation for what it was—Gideon protecting me, setting order in his pack without taking a life because he saw the fear in my eyes. But I can't let myself see it like that. I can't fall in love with him just to watch him die.

"I don't think anyone outside of the pack would know." Mila's soft voice breaks me out of my thoughts again, and she smiles at me. "Hell, I don't think most of the pack even knows. Just those of us who actually pay attention to our alpha." She points her fork at my untouched plate. "Eat up, girl. I made enough for thirds, and you're going to need it."

I bite into a piece of bacon with a curious glance at her. "Need it for what?"

Her smile spreads, both cheeks' dimples deepening. "I thought you might appreciate some training."

Standing in the middle of Gideon's back yard, just inside the tree line, I close my eyes and try to control my breathing, but after being out here for two hours already, I'm panting. I've never felt so out of shape.

"Again," Mila says. "Pull your wolf to the surface, just enough to lengthen your claws, and then hold it."

I nod, keeping my eyes closed and concentrating on the inner presence swirling just out of reach. Frustrated, I try to draw on my wolf, who's still annoyed with me from earlier.

*Admit he only wants to protect us. He chose not to kill that asshole in the bar for you, princess.*

The nickname is spat at me, an insult more than anything, and her irritation is palpable, mixing with my own.

"Again, Addy, come on!" Mila yells.

"I'm trying," I snap.

"Stop trying and *demand* it. This is *your* wolf. *Your* body. You tell her what to do, not the other way around."

My wolf laughs at her words, evading me again as I reach out to pull her forward. A frustrated growl comes from my lips.

*Just say it.*

Mila's voice is suddenly in my ear, making me jump. "You know, one time Aramin was caught sleeping with Gideon in his office."

In the blink of an eye, my wolf rushes to the surface. The force of the shift steals my breath.

"Don't let her take full control. Stop the shift." Her voice is farther away now, and I'm wondering how she's able to move so swiftly without me noticing or picking up her scent.

Shaking my head, I refocus, trying to stop the shift, but the image of Aramin wrapped in Gideon's arms on the same cot I laid beside him on burns in my mind.

"Don't let Aramin have more control over your wolf than you."

I let out a scream, releasing every piece of tension in my body with the sound, then take a few deep breaths. Gideon's initial training comes back to me, and the memory of his hands on my skin soothes the roiling emotions surging through me. I consciously relax each muscle in my body, shoving my wolf down further with each breath. Afterwards, calmness envelops me, and I open my eyes.

Mila stares back at me, pride beaming in her expression as she smiles at me. "You did it!"

I glance down to see claws where my nails used to be, elongated and sharp, and let the sense of accomplishment wash over me.

"I don't know what you did there in the end, but it was perfect." She walks over and lifts one of my hands, looking at my claws with fascination. "Do that every time, and you should be able to break into control effortlessly!"

I laugh nervously, not wanting to admit that the thought of being in Gideon's arm is the one thing that helps both me and my wolf calm down.

My wolf's bitter laugh echoes in my mind. *Because he is there for us when we need him, whether you admit it or not, princess.*

## CHAPTER TWO
*Gideon*

I TUG AT THE COLLAR OF MY SHIRT, WISHING I didn't have to be trapped in this godsforsaken room. The council holds all their meetings at the same place—the lodge. It's what the local humans would think is an exclusive, members-only club, secluded in the middle of the woods at the northern Vermont border. The large, dark oak building has walls of windows that reflect the forest when looking at them from the outside, but when looking out from within, the view is breathtaking. Large oaks, evergreen pines, and maple trees with knotted branches reach high into the sky, their branches interweaving to create an intricate canopy overhead. Mountains in the distance can be seen through the barren branches this time of year, and the occasional wildlife walking through the woods brings a calming sense of seclusion.

Adara would love it here... if it weren't for these pompous assholes surrounding the table and killing the mood. Then again—a smirk breaks across my face—if she's as feisty with them as she always is with me, it'd be far worth the entertainment.

"Disantollo?" Rathmann snaps, his voice laced with impatience.

I stare out the window for a few moments more, purposely making him wait to gain my attention.

Rathmann slams his fist down on the conference table—a large and round one with chairs crowded around, one for each councilman plus an extra for me. "We demand an answer for your insolent crimes. The disrespect of allowing this *witch*—" he spits out, as I cut him off.

"I'm sorry, you were saying something?" I lazily bring my gaze from his fist sitting in a small hole within the table to his face, the fury written across his expression making the veins in his neck bulge.

Raymond Grant, the highest ranking councilman, clears his throat. "Rathmann was saying that you've not only bitten—and changed—a witch, but you've also allowed her to live."

"Hmm. I do remember something along those lines." I rest my elbow on the arm of my chair, rubbing a finger over my chin.

"Well?" Grant cocks a brow.

"Was there a question in there I'm supposed to answer? Sounds as though you've already done your research." Leaning back in my seat, I bring my gaze back to the forest, far preferring to enjoy the view of the forest than entertain the pissing contest at the table.

Rathmann starts to say something, but Grant raises a hand, quieting him instantly. "So, this is true?" Grant asks, his lips pressed into a firm line. "And you've yet to take care of the issue?"

A bark of laughter escapes me. "Take care of the *issue*? You mean kill her just to sate your insecurities that a woman might become powerful enough to dethrone you all?" My laughter grows. "If there weren't so many aspects of your politics I sorely hated, I would've dethroned you myself years ago, and you all know it. It's the only reason you haven't *taken care* of me after all these centuries. *Because you can't.*"

Standing, I straighten my button up, hating the formalities of these meetings. The smile falls from my face as I meet the eyes of each councilman before me, all eight of them a personal thorn in my side.

"I'll be going now, but I want you to remember," my gaze lands on Rathmann, lingering for a second longer than the rest before moving to Grant, "any threat to my pack, especially my mate, is a direct threat to myself, and I don't take to those kindly. As you're well aware. Let this second, *generous* warning be the final warning you gentlemen need."

Grant's eyes narrow, and Rathmann gapes at me, shock written clearly on his face for a moment before his jaw clenches. "*Mate?*" Rathmann spits. "You mated with that mongrel hybrid?"

I dart forward, my hand wrapping around his throat. We're similar in height, but I lift him easily onto the tips of his toes, his face hovering a few inches above mine. "Don't *ever*," I whisper, my eyes searing into his, "talk about her like that again. Don't talk about her *at all*." I throw him down to the ground, waiting a moment as he glares up at me. Spinning on my heel, I walk back to the front of the room.

Frank steps forward from where he'd been standing behind my chair, a deep growl coming from his chest as his eyes flick to silver. I turn and quirk an eyebrow at Rathmann, who's now on his feet with a red handprint around his throat, and smirk when Grant holds his hand up at him again.

I fix the collar of my shirt and smooth my hands down the front of it. "Great speaking with you, councilmen. Next time, try an email. It'll save some time." Frank trails behind me as we walk through the thick oak doors, letting them slam shut behind us.

As we make our way to the black sedan parked in the circular drive, I curse the fact that I chose to drive here, knowing I could've saved at least fifteen minutes by shifting and racing through the forest. But these council meetings demand appearances, especially for the occasional mundane human who 'walks the trails,' hoping to get a glimpse of the lodge and its 'members.'

I stare out the window as Frank drives, my mind drifting to Adara, the little lycan witch that's stolen everyone's attention. Is she awake now? Is she disappointed that I'm not there to be with her? The image of her wrapped in my t-shirt this morning before I left with Frank pops into my mind, her dark hair draped over the pillowcases as light snores escaped her.

Frank clears his throat, and I glance at him, annoyed he interrupted my thoughts. "Was that the best decision? Announcing that she's your mate?" His gaze flicks to mine before returning to the road in front of him.

"It was the best choice, given their concern over her powers." I shrug, gazing out the window at the trees racing by.

His brows furrow. "Won't they be even more concerned knowing she's your mate?"

A dark chuckle escapes me. "Yes, but they'll also be more afraid. As my mate, our power will be shared between us, making each of us stronger. At least now she's under my protection."

Mates aren't as common as they used to be, with the wolf packs as large as they've grown now. They're harder to find, and the knowledge and stories surrounding them have died down a bit. Even in my own pack, there's only a small handful who have mated, and the one time I saw a bond stronger than any other was Jaz's parents... The memory of Bella's death, her pain and the way she couldn't bear to live without a scum like Sawyer, makes me wonder what it would be like to suffer the loss of a mate I actually enjoy being around...

"And as my mate, she'll be more vital to me, more protected, and more avenged if they dare to attempt anything," I whisper, trying to push the thought of anyone hurting Adara from my mind.

*They wouldn't dare*, my wolf growls.

And I have to admit, I hope he's right.

The drive home is long—far longer than I have the patience for, and I struggle against the urge to tell Frank to pull over so I can run the rest of the way back. It's nearly dinnertime when we pull into town, driving past the bar's empty lot.

My wolf paces inside me, anxious to see our mate after the events of the night before—after searching for her endlessly with a weakening bond between us, just to have her appear injured on our doorstep. My jaw ticks at the thought of her wounds, but it's the next image—of her wet hair dripping onto the floor as it hangs over her shoulders, with a towel wrapped tightly around her, clinging to every curve—that sends my wolf into a frenzy. My claws lengthen, and it's all I can do to focus on not tearing the sedan's doors from their hinges as we pull into the driveway of my house.

I barely notice Frank's smirk as I burst from the car and cross the front yard. Trees loom in the distance as a backdrop against the dark house. I reach for the front door when a light laugh hits my ears, and I quickly spin around to walk to the back of my property.

Adara sits beside the fireplace, her legs pulled up onto the seat. Her cheeks are red from the slight chill in the late September air, and her raven sits perched on her shoulder. Within moments, I find myself standing before her, her lips parted in surprise as she gazes up at me, and I drown in her violet eyes. A small smile tugs at my mouth when I think of how I thought they were blue just a couple of weeks ago—a color I could never picture them being now.

Leaning forward, I cup her jaw in one hand and hold her gaze, waiting for her to pull away, but she doesn't. She melts into me, and I barely register the ruffle of feathers just before I touch my lips to her.

A small cough comes from my left, and I snarl as I break our kiss, scooping Adara up into my arms and spinning to sit in the lounge chair with her nestled on my lap. Her cheeks flame, and I smirk, catching Mila's teasing glance thrown at Adara. "Comfy, little witch?" I whisper against her hair.

She audibly swallows, nodding slightly, then turns her head to glare at me when I chuckle. Frank wraps an arm around Mila's waist as they stand by the grill, asking her about whatever food she's cooking. Inhaling deeply, I let the mouthwatering scent of steaks swirl around me.

"Steak?" I raise a brow at Adara.

She smiles. "Yeah, Mila has been cooking all day. Everything she's made so far has been delicious."

I chuckle again. "Made a new friend then?"

She snaps her gaze to mine, her furrowed brows betraying the war going on inside her head.

"It's alright to make friends. We're all pack here." I rub my thumb over her hip where my hand lays. "Relax, *mia fiamma*."

Chewing on her lip, she glances briefly down at mine before turning back to Mila and Frank standing before the grill. "I've never had a friend before that wasn't Kaylus or Jules. I'm not sure how to do that. Make friends."

"You're already doing it," I say, noticing how Mila smiles at us as she rests her head on Frank's shoulder.

Adara nods again, but the tightness in my chest lingers. What kind of monster of a mother never lets her child have an actual friend in life? I inhale slowly through my nose, keeping my anger in check so I don't accidentally dig my claws into her hip. The thin material of her leggings between us is enough to drive my wolf wild in a whole other way, though, and I have to work to focus on anything but the weight of her in my lap, the feel of her body heat seeping into my skin, the scent of this forest nymph sitting so close to me.

## CHAPTER THREE
*Adara*

GIDEON'S HAND DOESN'T MOVE, HIS THUMB rubbing against the curve of where my thigh meets my hip, sending a series of sparks through my body. It feels so right to be sitting in his lap, which makes me feel like a traitor. Why is it so hard to hate him when I've seen his temper, his violence?

I know he's my mate, but does that mean I just ignore everything else? His past? His cruelty? Every red flag?

My wolf growls at my train of thought, and I try to ignore her.

*He's never been violent with us, though, has he? He only protects us.*

Chewing on the inside of my cheek, I blow out a breath. That is true, but—

*And your coven hasn't helped you or Jules in all the years you've been loyal. Gideon and his pack have, and they've never demanded anything but your silence.*

I shake my head to clear the thoughts. My wolf isn't helping, and I just need her to shut up and leave me alone.

*No. I won't leave you alone until you accept him.*

"Are you okay?" Gideon's gravelly voice is next to my ear, his lips grazing the tip of it, and I jump at the sudden intimacy.

"Yeah, fine," I say, shooting off his lap. "I, uh, just need a drink." I move toward the kitchen, but he grabs my wrist.

"I'll get it. I need to get out of these clothes anyway." He guides me back to the lounge chair, pushing my shoulders down gently until I sit.

I fidget on the seat, wanting the release of movement to clear my mind, but as I watch him walk away, I drink him in. His wavy black hair is slicked back, and the suit he wears clings to every curve of muscle. His jacket is stretched tight across his broad shoulders, the sleeves straining against his biceps, and pants grip his hips and backside the way I wish my hands were able to. I lick my lips and blush as he glances over his shoulder, his eyebrow arching over his stormy gray eyes.

Looking away quickly, I find Mila standing by the grill still with Frank, and I try—and fail—to think of something to ask them, feeling like my brain is broken after the Gideon overload.

"So." Mila plops down onto the chair beside me, smiling from ear to ear as she watches Frank walk inside through the slider doors. "That was some kinda hello!"

My cheeks flame again at the memory—and the embarrassment of knowing it was witnessed.

She laughs, the sound pulling a smile from my lips despite myself. "Gods, you are so lucky. I haven't seen Gideon this happy... *ever*."

I give a small laugh. "Ever? How long have you known him?"

"Oh, maybe a century now?" She shrugs as I stare at her, my mouth hanging open. "I used to keep to myself, though. I've only just started going to the bar and hanging out in the last few months. Frank is just..." She bites her lower lip and smiles.

"He is really sweet," I say with a smile. "Honestly, I'm still surprised by how nice you guys are to me, and the age concept is still a bit... strange."

"We may bite when we want to, but we're nothing to worry about." She winks, getting up to flip the steaks on the grill. "And," she calls over her shoulder, "you'll get used to the age part with some time, now that you have plenty of it."

It takes a moment to dawn on me—I'm immortal. Being a wolf, I'm now immortal and have all the time in the world. Instead of being excited about the fact, dread creeps up around me, shrouding around my shoulders like an itchy wool shawl. What about Jules? Will I have to watch her grow old and die? Does Kaylus become immortal as my familiar?

Glancing over my shoulder into the tree branches behind me, I see Kaylus's sleek black form, his beak craned around and nestled under his wing as he sleeps. As my familiar, he's able to share certain powers with me—such as telepathy—but also life force. We can share the life force drawn between the two of us, always knowing where the other is and if they're wounded. If I were to be on the brink of death, he could share his life force with me to help me survive, and I could do the same for him. But with my life force being an endless stream of immortality now, does that mean his is too, or will he die and leave me without the one friend I've been able to rely upon?

My breathing quickens, and my vision begins to tunnel. My world was so small, filled with just a couple of loved ones and the purpose of sending Jules to the academy, but now I feel cursed to watch everything crumble around me as time picks them off one by one—or as Monique does in an effort to kill or steal my wolf.

I close my eyes against the panic, tears burning behind my eyelids, my throat becoming tight. Focusing, I try to concentrate on my breathing, but every breath brings an image of death.

Jules, attacked by Monique, tortured and dying because of me.

Kaylus, blood soaking his sleek black feathers. Gideon...

A hand touches my chest, gently but steadily applying pressure just below my collarbone. "Breathe, *mia fiamma*. In—one, two, three. Out—one, two, three."

My eyes fly open and find his, calm rainstorms staring back at me, brows furrowed with concern as he kneels before me.

His thumb swipes my cheek, wiping away a tear that escaped, as he looks me over briefly. "Are you alright?"

I let him wrap his arms around me, crushing my face against his shirt as I inhale his scent. As his cologne invades my senses, my muscles relax, and I nod against his chest. The sound of gravel crunching has his arms tensing before he relaxes again. I peek around his shoulder to find an older woman with gray streaked black hair walking around the side of the house with a small brown haired girl following her.

"Maddie!" Mila says, rushing over to take the large casserole dish from her hands.

"I hope you don't mind, but we brought some potato salad." The older woman smiles, her gaze sweeping the yard briefly. "If I'm not mistaken, it'll pair wonderfully with those grilled steaks." She winks at Mila before making her way over to us, sitting herself down on the chair beside us. "Well, Gideon, don't just sit there. Introduce me to this beautiful woman."

My cheeks heat at the compliment, and I tuck a strand of hair behind my ears. "Adara," I say, reaching out my hand. "It's nice to meet you..." I trail off, realizing I'm not sure if I should call her by the nickname as Mila did.

She smiles, a glint in her eyes. "Madrona, but you're welcome to call me Maddie if you'd like."

Gideon shuffles to sit on the chair, pulling me onto his lap as before, and I fight against the blush flaming my cheeks again. "Madrona is the pack mother. One of many pack parents, but easily the best." He gives her a warm smile, the rare expression stealing my breath as it transforms his face. "That's Jaz," he nods to the brown haired girl standing by the grill, glaring at Frank with her hands on her hips as he laughs. "Sawyer and Bella's girl," he adds under his breath.

It takes me a minute to work through the familiarity of that first name, but slowly, the pieces click together in my mind. The blue book in his office. Sawyer. I twist around. "But... her mother..."

"She killed herself a few years after his death," he answers.

My eyes travel back to the spitfire girl before me. Pride and strength ooze from her small frame, but my heart breaks for her all the same.

"She's been doing very well since you found her," Madrona says. "She won't talk about that night, but whatever you did... Gideon, you saved her."

His lips press into a firm line. "She never needed saving. She just needed to remember where she came from."

Madrona nods, the shadow of a smile ghosting her lips.

I make a mental note to ask him more about it later when everyone else leaves.

"I think I'll go help Mila with the food." Madrona pushes herself up from the chair, making her way to Mila and following her into the kitchen.

Not long after she walks inside, Jaz skips over from the grill and takes her seat. "Found her then?" she says, smirking.

Gideon rolls his eyes.

Jaz laughs. "He was going *feral* trying to find you."

He cuts his gaze to her with a glare, which only makes her laugh harder.

"He almost gave up. Can you believe that?"

I look over my shoulder at Gideon behind me, feeling his fingers tighten on my hips. "You almost gave up?"

"I did not—"

Jaz nods, her eyes alight with mischief as she cuts him off. "Your scent was making the hunters go in circles. It was driving him straight *feral*."

"The hunters?" I ask, unsure what that means. Did Gideon have his entire pack searching for me?

"Oh, yeah." Jaz leans back on the lounge chair. "He had the hunters out, the whole pack on high alert. He was even out there tracking you himself, which happens *never*. I tried to help, but," she shrugs and rolls her eyes, "you know how stubborn he is."

A laugh escapes me at her attitude—so carefree and relaxed while insulting the most dangerous wolf in existence. One look at Gideon tells me he doesn't actually mind, despite the gruff exterior.

"You had school. You can't just skip your studies to prance around like—"

"Yeah, yeah, *Dad*." She waves her hand in his direction.

"You're insufferable," he growls.

She ignores him, jumping forward to sit on the edge of the chair. "Oh! Can you do magic? I'd love to see it. Does being a witch help you control your wolf better? I can shift on demand now, but it's still not the most comfortable."

I laugh as the questions tumble out of her. Licking my lips, I say a silent prayer to Hecate that I won't accidentally melt anything this time and hold out my hand, palm up. Pink sparks dance along my fingertips, and a smile breaks across my face as Jaz squeals.

"That is so wicked! What else can you do? Can you do any spells on stuff? Can you use magic while you're a wolf?"

"I'm actually still learning about my wolf... and my magic." I frown at my hands as I let the sparks fizzle out, studying my palms for a moment before glancing back up at her. "But Mila was helping me train today."

"You should come to the training classes!" she says, excited. "Darrold is training all of us new to shifting in the pack again tomorrow. It—"

"No," Gideon says flatly.

Jaz narrows her gaze at him. "Why? And if it's some dumb reason like training her yourself, you better not even bother. You can still train her. The classes could be extra. And being in a group, to feel like part of our pack, would be *good* for her."

His jaw flexes as he clenches his teeth. I put my hands over his where they sit on my hips, rubbing my thumb along the back of his hands. "It would be helpful, I think. And I'd like to meet more of the pack as an equal."

He searches my eyes, the frown never leaving his lips.

"And if you say no again," I add, raising a brow at him, "I'll go and just not tell you."

Jaz laughs, making Gideon glare at her briefly. "Oh, I like her," she manages to say between breaths.

"Dinner!" Mila calls from the slider door.

Jaz shoots up from the chair, skipping into the house. I get up to follow her, but Gideon quickly pulls me back down, his hand cupping my cheek. "You're as insufferable as that pup, but gods, are you beautiful when you have that defiant fire dancing in your eyes."

I glance away briefly, my mind still stuck on what Madrona mentioned before. "What did she mean earlier? When Madrona said you saved her?"

His eyes travel lazily up from my lips. "Like I said, Jaz never needed me to save her. I only reminded her of where she came from."

Scowling at him, I sigh. "That doesn't actually answer anything."

He chuckles. "Darling, it answers everything." He presses his lips softly to mine before pulling back. "Come on, let's get inside before they come searching for us."

I laugh as he sets me on my feet with a huff, his hand never letting go of mine as we walk around the fireplace and into the house.

It never occurs to me that when we're together, the demons screaming in my mind that I'm betraying my coven are silent, the voice that sounds like Monique telling me I'm worthless has nothing to say. As long as Gideon is touching me, everything else falls away, and I've never felt lighter.

## CHAPTER FOUR
*Gideon*

FRANK'S LAUGH BOOMS ACROSS THE TABLE, HIS eyes dancing with mirth as he looks at Mila. Gods, I've never seen him so happy in the centuries he's stood by my side. My gaze sweeps across the table, glancing over Jaz lighting up the room with her smile, and lands on Adara next to me. She watches those around the table with a mixture of curiosity and joy, but a hint of doubt plays on her features.

*You love her*, my wolf says, startling me. His voice sounds strange, distant.

She's my mate.

*Yes, but it's more than that. You actually love this witch.* He laughs, the sound distorted as if underwater.

You told me to accept the mate bond. You—

*I didn't expect you to love her, this witch that could bring death to our entire pack. She'll become more powerful than us once she awakens her true powers, and then what? You can't use her witch powers like she can use your wolf abilities.*

A lead weight settles in my gut at those words. More powerful than me? Can I trust her to protect us, from both witch and wolf alike, when I can't be a safeguard against her? Because they will attack—every side will attack to gain that kind of power. The image of Adara, silhouetted against a raging fire behind her, flits across my mind.

"Are you okay?"

Blinking, I focus back on Adara sitting beside me, her brows furrowed in concern as she places her hand atop mine.

*She'll kill us all.*

"Gideon?" she whispers.

I nod and jerk my hand from her grasp. "Fine."

Her lips press into a firm line, and I fight the urge to run my thumb along them until they relax beneath my touch. But my head feels foggy, and I can't think straight. Images of Grace and Ella race through my mind—the flames licking at the night sky as they swallowed my family and our home, followed by Adara on the night she came to me—soot and ash coating her hair and fingers.

The rest of dinner goes by in a blur, my mood souring by the minute, until finally everyone stands to leave. Adara says goodnight and heads up to her room, one last glance thrown over her shoulder in my direction as I walk them to the door. I try to ignore the tightness in my chest at the confusion written across her face.

"Gideon." Madrona stops me as I move to close the door behind her, the others already halfway to their cars. She smiles when I raise my brows at her. "Grace and Ella were beautiful lights in your darkness. Do your best to not squelch the few lights you have left." Reaching up to pat my cheek, she looks over my shoulder at the stairs. "Love can make the fiercest of protectors."

She moves to leave, and I can't help but watch her go, her long hair swaying with each step. After a moment, I shake my head to clear it and go inside. Grabbing the whiskey from the liquor cabinet and throwing myself down onto the sofa with a sigh, I take a pull from the bottle and stare at the ceiling.

She's up there. In a bed in my house—*alone*. I hate being on a different floor from her, but if I were to go to my own room, I'd be across the house. I don't know which is worse—the aching desire to be near her or the blinding panic in my head every time I think of her fire. Gods, why is this so difficult? Why did the fates damn me with this witch?

Groaning, I take another pull from the bottle, letting the amber liquid warm its way down my throat. I snatch the black journal off the side table, knowing Frank left it here for me on purpose.

"*A pack issue,*" he'd said. "*Read it when you're alone.*"

Cracking open the journal, the first few words swim before me, rage coloring my vision.

*There's been talk of challenging you for alpha...*

"Aaron Kilch," I read the name outloud like a curse before throwing the journal across the room. The spine smacks into the wall, and it drops to the floor. I throw back another gulp of liquor, waiting for my wolf to calm down before I hunt Aaron down tonight and tear him apart the way I should've that night he laid his hands on Adara.

I should've killed him then.

*You would've terrified her even more.*

"I don't care," I grumble, scowling at the floor at the sound of his voice—clear, crisp, as if he were right next to me. "If she can't stomach how I handle my pack, then she has no place beside me, leading it."

I storm over to the wall and leaf through the rest of the journal before tossing it back on the table and heading upstairs. I need sleep before dealing with this, especially after that shitstorm of a council meeting. Rathmann's burning gaze enters my mind, and I smirk. I tried playing nice, but he's set on bringing his own destruction.

Padding up the stairs, I walk down the hall, pausing briefly outside Adara's door. My fist hovers in the air, wanting to knock, but something stops me. Her lights are off. Is she asleep already or just laying there in the dark? Clenching my jaw, I shove my fist into my pants pocket and continue walking to my own door.

Why did I have to buy such a big godsforsaken house? It couldn't have been a one bedroom, where the only option she would've had is to sleep beside me. My hands ache to hold her tight against me, like when we laid on the cot in my office, yet... another part of me craves the distance between us.

When I got home, I couldn't think of anything except seeing her, touching her. But... when I saw her through the window, after going inside to change out of my suit, I almost couldn't bear to go back outside to her. It was only after seeing her out there—breathing rapidly with her eyes squeezed tightly shut, panic radiating from her whole body and throbbing through our bond—that I couldn't keep myself from her any longer. I found myself standing beside her before I even realized my feet were moving, reaching out to touch her chest without a second though. Once I did, it was as if the rest of the world fell away. I didn't want to ever take my hand from her again.

Now, climbing into bed, my temples throb, fighting between the urge to carry her from the spare room and into my bed and the uneasy feeling that's been lingering in my head every time I step away from her. How do I protect my pack from a fate that seems unavoidable? From a fate that I don't know if I have the strength to walk away from, even if I had to...

*The bar is packed tonight. Almost the entire pack is here, but I don't understand why. The full moon happened two weeks ago, so it doesn't make sense for everyone to be this rowdy.*

*I melt into the shadows, walking along the edge of the crowded space and seeing if Kilch dared to show his face here tonight. Unable to see or smell him, I lean back against my office door, staying hidden in the corner by the bar.*

*"He ain't here," Frank says, pouring another round of beers for a few girls that hang around Mila.*

*I grunt. "That's obvious."*

*He chuckles and shakes his head, moving down the bar and filling drinks as he goes.*

*My eyes sweep the room again. Something feels off, but I can't put my finger on it. A rush of cold air prickles goosebumps along my arm, and I look over as a dark-haired woman enters the bar.*

*Adara?*

*But when she turns, it isn't her. Instead, it's one of the girls from Darrold's new group of shifters... but I can't remember her name.*

*Frustrated, I whirl around and throw my office door open. Where is Adara? I thought she was... coming here? Is that right? Is she still training with me?*

*I slump into the desk chair, rummaging around until I find the bottle of whiskey stashed under my desk. Without looking down, I lean back in my chair and take a pull from the bottle—gagging immediately. I quickly realize the liquid is wrong. It's not whiskey—it's thick, metallic. Glancing at the glass bottle, I watch the normally amber liquid swirling around, seeing that it's a deep red, so deep it's almost black. I swipe the back of my hand across my lips, the skin coming away tinged red with blood, and stumble out of the chair.*

*Backing away from the desk, I lose my balance and catch myself on the edge of the bookcase—the one by the window, but it isn't my reflection I see in the glass pane.*

*"Rathmann," I growl, reaching down to throw the window open. I want to tear the smug look right off his face, but the window is locked. Frustrated, I touch the metal lock—and hiss at the white hot pain erupting along my fingers. The metal is red, glowing, and hot as fuck. Blisters swell on my fingertips, and I snap my eyes back to Rathmann.*

*His smirk grows as he dangles something from his hand. Dark shadows dance under his eyes. Squinting into the night, I try to make out what he's holding... A raven, limp and swaying, hangs from his hard grip on the bird's feet—dead. Blood runs over his fingers, trailing down the bird's black feathers and dripping off its beak. Rage boils inside me at the image of Kaylus's body in this asshole's hand. Rathmann laughs, the smudges of blood and the talon scratches on his cheeks stretching.*

*A woman's scream echoes around me, and my blood runs cold, the cord in my chest tugging taut.*

*Adara.*

*Without a thought, I throw my elbow through the glass, trying to escape and save her. She has to be in trouble. Rathmann must have someone out there, someone who got to her while he—-*

*Smoke billows into my office through the hole I've made, and I stagger back, coughing and waving my hand in front of my face, but the smoke chokes me, relentless. Turning around, I bolt to the office door, but the minute I grab the doorknob, the metal sears into my palm. Snarling, I kick the door open, holding my hand to my chest and cursing whatever magic this is that's causing these burns.*

*"Fuck," I whisper, frantically searching the bar, but the dense crowd is hazy—and panicked.*

*"Gideon!" Frank yells from the other end of the bar.*

*The bar is in an uproar, people screaming as flames lick at the walls all around, blocking every exit. Wood beams creak and snap beneath the bright orange flames, and I dive forward, knocking Mila out of the way of a falling piece of the ceiling. Tears trail through the soot covering her face, and I yell for Frank as he barrels through the crowd to us. He gathers Mila in his arms, swiping his thumbs across her cheeks to wipe away her tears, and I have to look away, guilt and jealousy warring inside me. I've done this—I brought this death to my pack's front door by protecting her, protecting Adara.*

*I have to find her.*

*I rush behind the bar, grabbing the crowbar I keep hidden under the liquor shelves and opening a hidden door in the floorboards. Why didn't Frank do this already? I curse under my breath as I reach in to grab the two fire extinguishers I have stashed away down there, but my hand touches nothing but air. Pushing back the questions in my mind, I move forward to open the damn doors. I throw the crowbar into the crack between the metal doors, busting open one side, then the* other. Smoke follows me out the door as I stumble outside, followed by waves of people stampeding out of the burning building.

Coughing, my eyes burning, I search for Adara. Of all the times, why is my wolf silent now? Why can't I feel her?

I bolt around the building, keeping my distance from the popping embers as the flames eat away at my bar, and find Rathmann laying on the ground—Adara standing above him. The councilman's face is soaked in blood, his clothes on fire as he screams—the sound like knives in my ears. Flames lick at Adara's arms, her hair floating around her head as if she were underwater, the tips a flickering orange like the embers of a fire.

A hoarse scream bursts from her lips, and she holds her flame-laced palms out to Rathmann, who scoots back on the ground, terror painting his face. "Please," he rasps. "Please! Don't!"

"You don't get to ask me favors, wolf!" she hisses, and even her voice is different, crackling and haunting.

Another beam snaps in the bar, and I duck my head at the noise, finally breaking from my trance. "Adara, wait!" I yell.

Her face snaps toward me, and my heart stops. Her eyes—usually violet as a dark twilight sky or silver like the stars above—now glow, flames licking the black pits of her pupils.

I jolt awake, my hand flying to my chest. My heart hammers against my palm.

It was just a dream. A dream... more like a gods damn nightmare.

*Right, just a dream,* my wolf says sarcastically.

"I can't deal with you right now," I mumble under my breath, swinging my legs over the side of the bed and resting my head in my hands. My body still trembles, and the sheets are sticking to me, soaked in sweat. I focus on my breathing, forcing the image of Adara, consumed by fire magic, out of my mind. After a few unsuccessful attempts to clear my head, I shove up from the bed and walk out of my room. I briefly pause by her door again, almost needing to check to make sure she's safe—in her bed and safe from her magic—but I shake my head. Black pits where eyes should be, filled with a raging fire, blink across my mind's eye, and I stumble away from her door. I make my way downstairs, running into the woods, stripping my sweatpants off as I go.

A run will do me some good to clear my head.

## CHAPTER FIVE
*Adara*

I HOLD MY BREATH AS I HEAR GIDEON'S DOOR open not long after he shut it. His footsteps pad down the hall and pause before my door, just as he did when he went into his room. A part of me wishes he would just open the door and come in here—whether to kiss me or talk to me, I don't care. After the way he shut me out at dinner, I'm struggling against the urge to go to him. Is he okay? Did something happen at the council meeting that he didn't tell me about?

But when he got home from that meeting, he was fine. He was... normal, affectionate, *hot*. I lift my hands and cover my face. When did I start thinking of that as normal? And when did I start wanting him to touch me the way he did tonight despite the risks, the obvious trouble that it'd be asking for?

But the way he looked at me at the table—with mistrust and fear—breaks my heart again just remembering it. All the warmth had left my body when he pulled his hand from mine, and I hate that. I never wanted to like him, let alone be his mate. The only way this will end is in pain—Monique will make sure of that, not to mention the wolf council *and* my coven. Was Monique right about Batya's prophecy? But how could I reign over everyone when I can't control either of my powers, let alone be powerful enough to make anyone listen to me?

Sighing, I roll over and face the window. I left it cracked open so Kaylus could fly in to the nest I made him beside the bed. I reach out and stroke along his sleek feathers, smiling at the thought that he can finally be a true familiar—one that never leaves my side, morning or night, instead of being cast outside into the shadows, a hidden secret. My gaze travels down to the nightstand, the square silver device sitting there. Chloe, Monique's office assistant, had sent it back with Kaylus last night, instructing him to not give it to me until I was alone. It has a small window where texts can appear. If I hold it in my hands and concentrate on the message I want to send, it'll absorb that through the enchantment seared into it, then send it to the sibling device that Jules has.

*Safe*, she wrote to me. *Love you.*

*Love you*, I wrote back, tears pricking at my eyes.

Another wave of emotion overtakes me, thankful to have Chloe on our side through this chaos. I can only hope the coven will understand Jules had nothing to do with this—my wolf betrayal—and allow her to attend the academy. Maybe I can talk to Gideon about working at the bar to continue saving up to pay her tuition. If the academy doesn't know where it came from, they shouldn't ask any questions... I hope.

A breeze picks up through the window, and Gideon's scent wafts into my room—cedarwood and caramel... I frown. And a small touch of mint? Aramin's red hair flashes through my mind, and I get out of bed quietly, stepping toward the window. Gideon's black wolf rushes into the forest—alone. My brows pull down as I chew on my lower lip. There was a vague minty smell at the dinner table tonight. Could that have been him? Could it have been *her*—did he see her on his way back?

My nails lengthen into claws, carving into the wood windowsill as a searing jealousy blooms in my chest. I try to shake the thought from my mind. It shouldn't matter who he sees or what he does. He isn't mine.

*Yes, he is. He is faithfully ours,* my wolf says.

I scoff at her words and roll my eyes. It doesn't matter because he won't be ours for long. Once I get back to Lockwood Forest, I can find that witch and then the well. Then, we won't have a mate, and maybe everything can go back to normal.

*Back to normal? To the abuse of the woman who wants to kill you?* My wolf laughs, mocking me, and I clench my jaw.

"Oh, just shut up," I whisper. I hold back the crushing weight of sorrow, knowing normal will never come back. My home is gone, my mother will never stop trying to kill me, and my coven may never accept me back, even if I get rid of my wolf. But as a witch, the wolf council will never accept me, either. I have nowhere to go... nowhere to belong.

*You belong here, with Gideon.*

Groaning, I run my hands through my hair and pull it into a bun on the top of my head before sinking down onto the bed. If I can't have normal back, then I can at least make a better future for Jules. Maybe Chloe needs a permanent roommate, even. I could live with her when I get my wolf under control—or gone. Jules can go to the academy. I can work with the humans, or maybe get my coven to believe I don't have a wolf. Monique never had any proof I could shift anyway, right? We can make a new normal—a *better* normal. Hope touches the edges of my mind, and a small smile lifts my lips.

It'll be fine. But first—training.

Sleep evades me all night, and I toss and turn in between studying the shadows playing along the ceiling. Sighing, I throw the covers off as the first rays of sun peek through the window. I never heard Gideon come back last night, so I don't bother pulling on my leggings, making my way downstairs in just his t-shirt. I yawn as I start a pot of coffee, the house quiet as the pot gurgles and the smell of caffeine permeates the space. Rubbing a hand over my face, I lean my elbow on the counter and rest my chin on my hand as I wait for it to finish brewing.

I quickly realize I don't know where the mugs are and start opening each cabinet. Scrunching up my face, I try to think back to Mila and where she got the glasses for breakfast yesterday, but I remember they were already sitting on the counter.

"You've got to be kidding," I mutter, coming up empty handed on the fourth cabinet. For a brief moment, I consider a finder's spell, but I dismiss it quickly. Knowing my luck, I'll melt the cabinets instead of just the coffee pot like the last time I used a more complicated spell.

"Top cabinet, on your right," a soft, husky voice says from the doorway.

I gasp and whirl around, finding Gideon leaning against the doorframe in sweatpants that hug his hips in a way that makes my wolf whimper inside. His hair is wet, as if he just showered, the dark waves pushed back from his face. The tanned skin of his bare arms and chest look so soft that I ache to run my fingers across them.

He chuckles, a smirk stretching across his mouth, as he catches my gaze.

Blushing fiercely, I turn back around. I start to reach for the cabinet he mentioned, but stop, realizing the t-shirt rides up to my waist when I reach for the top shelf. "Um…"

"I'll grab them." He comes into the kitchen, stepping behind me and pressing his body against my back, my stomach against the cold counter as his arm raises above my head to grab two mugs. "Here," he says into my ear, the vibration of his voice rumbling against me. He sets the mugs on the counter in front of me, his fingers grazing my wrist and traveling up to my elbow.

My breath hitches, and my heart plummets when he steps away, feeling the loss of the warmth of his body as he sits on a stool at the island. I glance over my shoulder and find him watching me, his gaze both hungry and… happy? My mind is spinning at the back and forth of his moods.

"Cream is in the fridge, and sugar is on the counter there," he says, motioning to the white ceramic jar in front of me.

I make my own coffee how I like it—medium brown and sweet—then turn and raise my brows at him with the second mug.

"Black."

I scrunch up my face. "Black?"

He chuckles as I set the full steaming cup before him. "I like my coffee strong and not diluted, just how I like… other things."

I break my gaze from his, trying to ignore the warmth that floods through me at his words as I move around the island to sit on the other stool beside him. I tug down the shirt to cover my thighs. "I didn't realize you were home."

He shrugs, lifting the mug to his lips and taking a sip. "I wasn't. I only just got back."

"But your hair is wet," I say, shooting him a look.

The corner of his mouth lifts again, his eyes finding mine. "Ever observant, little witch."

I scowl at him, choosing not to press the conversation further despite the desire to hear his voice.

After a few silent minutes, he drains the last of his coffee and rinses it out in the sink. He walks around the island, brushing past me on his way out of the kitchen. "If you're planning to go to Darrold's, you'll want to get dressed, *mia fiamma*."

"What does that mean?" I ask, staring at his broad shoulders as he walks away.

"It means get ready before you're late."

Glaring after him, I nurse the last few sips of my coffee before running upstairs and pulling on leggings and a new t-shirt from the pile of clothes Mila brought me yesterday and retying my bun.

It's my first time driving through town during the daylight hours. The forest is thick here, but the main road that leads through town is dotted with the occasional home, two-stories with wood siding. Most have large front lawns, some littered with children's toys. As we get further into town, it becomes more congested, and we turn at the only stoplight onto a street with a handful of almost identical homes—two-stories with a spattering of windows across the front facing walls, short gravel drives, and small covered porches. Pulling into the driveway of the white one, Gideon puts his truck in park.

"Here you are," he says. "Just walk around to the back yard."

"Wait, you're not coming?" For some reason, being here without him, in the middle of his pack, makes me feel more vulnerable than him walking in on me with no pants on this morning.

He reaches out to brush a stray strand of hair behind my ear. "The new shifters get nervous, so I don't watch them train. It can make it more difficult for them, and accidents happen when shifters get frustrated and lose control of their wolves. You'll be fine, *mia fiamma*."

I chew on my lip, looking from him to the edge of the house where it would lead to the back yard. "I thought you didn't want me to go."

"Mm, and I was told you'd go regardless." A glint flashes in his eyes. "At least now I know you've made it here safely. Though, if you're too afraid—"

I cut a look at him, and he laughs.

"Jaz will be there, so you won't be alone. And Darrold will play nice as long as you don't light his house on fire, little witch."

I heave a sigh. "Fine, but stop insulting me at every turn with your stupid nicknames." I push open the door and jump down from the truck. His bewildered expression almost makes me laugh as I slam the door behind me and walk toward the back of the house. That'll teach him for using his stupid little nicknames all the time. Gods only know what the one means that he keeps using today... me-something.

With each step toward the house, my amusement at finally having the last word with Gideon fades. My palms start to sweat, so I curl my fingers into fists, tugging the sleeves of my borrowed sweatshirt to my knuckles. Entering the back yard, my eyes glance over the group of maybe fifteen kids with one man at the center of them. He's tall, with a slim waist, and his blond hair looks like wheat in the early morning sun.

He must be Darrold.

I suck in a deep breath, steeling my nerves as I realize I don't know what Gideon told them about me. If anything.

A small form runs over to me, and I quickly recognize Jaz and her brown hair.

"You came," she says, smirking as she reaches out to take my hand.

I nod, letting her guide me to the edge of the group. Standing close to her, she only comes up to my shoulders, but her back is straight. She's commanding her presence on purpose, and I try to hide a smile at the thought when I see how dwarfed she is by the rest of the shifters here.

"As I was saying," Darrold says, his blue eyes catching my gaze as he gives a small nod to me, "today, we'll be working in pairs. I'll call you each over, one by one, to assess your skills personally. The next full moon is coming up, so we want to be ready."

A cheer comes from the group, making me jump, and Jaz laughs beside me. I nudge her with my shoulder and make a face. "Are you going to be my partner?"

She shakes her head. "No, I was going to work with Semira."

A lump forms in my throat, and I search the group for another person I might recognize as Jaz bursts into laughter again.

"I'm only kidding! Of course I'll be your partner. Come on!" She pulls me to the edge of the yard, facing me and squaring her shoulders.

I look around the group, seeing each paired set of shifters facing each other. "Wait, what are we—"

A small hand slaps my face, leaving a sharp stinging on my cheek.

"Hey! That hurt!" I rub the tender spot on my face.

"Tune into your wolf!" She rolls her eyes. "She should have natural instincts. You should've seen that coming."

"I wasn't even looking. Or ready!" I stare down at her with my hands on my hips. "You could've warned me."

A raven caws, and I search the branches above us until I find Kaylus. His laughter echoes in my mind. *"Oh, I like her."*

I glare up at him, and another slap cracks across my face. "Hey!" I put my palm to my hot cheek, glaring down at the small spitfire before me.

"Well! Why aren't you listening to your wolf? We're *natural fighters*," she huffs.

"I don't want to fight you. You're just a kid!"

"I'm a *wolf*. Don't be such a lummox and open your mind to *your* wolf." Jaz narrows her gaze at me, crossing her arms over her chest.

Sighing, I stop rubbing my cheek, the sting subsiding, and close my eyes. "I don't think I even know what a lummox is," I grumble, as I reach into myself to find my wolf's presence. She evades me, snarling.

Jaz's heel stomps onto my foot, and I growl at her, squeezing my eyes shut tighter.

Reaching out again, the scent of spruce and burning paper surrounds me just as my fingers brush against my wolf's fur. The back yard fades away—the scents, the sounds, everything melts into a winter forest. Snow blankets every branch and the ground below my feet as I spin in a circle.

"But it's only September..." I whisper. "Where the hell am I?"

*You're in my territory,* my wolf says. *The part of your soul that is mine. That is* me.

Clouds fill the sky above me, a hazy sun diffused behind the overcast fog. Birch and maple trees fill the space, dark green firs and pines mingled throughout as a splash of life to the barren winter landscape. "It's... beautiful here."

The black she-wolf darts between the trees like a shadow, stalking me through the brush as I stand in the middle of a small field. *Why do you refuse to see that this is what we could be?*

Confused, I tear my gaze from the trees to stare at the wolf's silhouette in the darkness of the forest. "Because together, we pose a threat to everyone. We have nothing, no one. We don't belong anywhere."

*We belong with Gideon. He's our mate, our one true mate. Together, we could rule. We could be more powerful than any other wolf or witch out there. Because we're* both. *If you could just accept me, we—*

"No," I say, putting two fingers to my temple. "W-we can't. We aren't powerful. We're weak. *I'm weak.* I don't stand a chance against the wolf council or the coven or my godsforsaken mother." I shake my head, a burning headache forming behind my eyes.

*Accept your life! Accept your power! This is your responsibility now, to bear the power that could save Gideon. That could save everyone!*

"No! This will only get everyone killed! Monique will kill him—and Jules. She'll kill everyone to get what she wants, and all she wants is *you!*"

The black wolf exits the trees, stalking toward me, her lips curled back in a snarl. *Accepting your power is the only way you'll grow strong enough to defeat her and save them. If you want to call upon me again, upon the powers you so desperately want yet refuse to acknowledge, you should consider what it is you're actually afraid of. Monique being who she's always been—evil, selfish,* predictable—*or the happiness you refuse to think you deserve, as if you only deserve it if you're strong with no weaknesses. Strength isn't measured by lack of weakness, princess. It's measured by resolve against those weaknesses to persevere.*

A loud whoosh makes my ears pop, and I try to cover them, but a blazing heat sears my skin. The forest erupts into flames, the fire licking at every tree, melting every inch of snow. A wolf howls in the distance, and somehow, I've never felt so cold. A hazy image of Gideon staggering toward a burning house in the middle of the forest fire enters my mind, and I try to push it away because it isn't real.

But it *looks* real. His screams of agony *sound* real, guttural, heart wrenching. Goosebumps scatter across my arms, and the piercing pain in my chest as he screams for Ella, for Grace, over and over and over, feels agonizingly *real*.

Squeezing my eyes shut, a scream escapes me as I will everything away. This winter wonderland burning up into a hellish nightmare. This pain. This heartache. This man haunting my every waking moment.

Another scream startles me, the voice terrified and not my own. My eyes snap open to find Jaz watching me with a look of horror on her face. I'm sitting on the ground before her, the grass around me burned and scorched. Reaching out to touch it, I notice my hands—wolf claws where my nails should be.

My gaze darts back up to Jaz. "Are... are you okay?" I ask, my voice hoarse, my eyes scanning her for burns or injuries.

She nods frantically, a small thrill passing across her face as Darrold rushes up behind her. "Gideon's on his way. Are you alright?" He bends down to check on Jaz, his hands resting on her shoulders. He glances over at me, eyes roaming over my body. "And you?"

I nod meekly, not sure what to say. Glancing around, I see the rest of the group is gone except for the three of us. My mouth goes dry. "Did... anyone..."

Darrold shakes his head. "Thankfully, you two were in the back, and I'm assuming it was your raven who scratched my car to set off the alarm and divert our attention." He grimaces.

I look into the trees, and Kaylus caws, flying down to settle on the burned grass by my hand. Swallowing hard, I look back to Darrold. "I'm sorry," I whisper. "I-I can pay for the damages and—"

He waves his hand at me, a soft smile revealing a dimple in one cheek. "Don't worry about it."

Tears prick at my eyes. There's no doubt he now knows exactly what I am, even if Gideon hadn't told him, and yet there's no malice in his eyes. Nothing but kindness and sympathy stare back at me.

A truck's engine rumbles down the street just before tires squeal into the driveway, and I quickly swipe away the tears as Jaz scoots over and grabs onto my hand, making the lump in my throat grow.

*This is true family*, my wolf says, but all I feel is grief at knowing I finally found people who could love me, and all I can give them in return is a death sentence.

## CHAPTER SIX
*Gideon*

I DON'T BOTHER SHUTTING MY DOOR AS I JUMP out of the truck and race around the house to the back yard. Darrold was cryptic on the phone, but the message was clear—Adara's magic came out during training, uncontrolled. I don't know the carnage I was expecting to see, but it definitely isn't the small ring of burned grass with an untouched Jaz sitting beside her, holding her hand.

My anger flares, and my glare lands on Darrold. "Didn't you say there were injuries or damage?" My tone is clipped as I talk to him, kneeling down to assess Jaz, then Adara, a blush lighting across Adara's face. Concern for her overpowers the smallest twinge of... something stirring in my chest, wanting me to back away from the witch who could burn everything to the ground.

"No, boss. I said I'm not sure on injuries and there's minimal damage." Darrold has enough sense to sound apologetic. "It looks like the training might've activated some witch magic. I didn't get to test her wolf yet, though her claws came out nicely along with the... uh... fire."

My eyes never leave her face, taking in every inch, every centimeter, until I know she's not hurt. Not physically anyway. I brush back the lock of hair that falls across her forehead, tucking it behind her ear, and she looks up at me from beneath her lashes. Violet eyes speckled with the silver of her wolf, like the few bright stars seen in a darkening twilight sky, stare back at me. And gods be damned, I don't know if I'll ever choose anything over her. My pack, my status, my own life... none of it compares to the witch sitting before me.

Cupping her cheek in my hand, a fog lifts from my mind, the twinge from earlier dissipates. Suddenly, I can't catch my breath. I want to drown in her. I want her very essence, her soul, to be so entwined with mine that we can't find where one of us ends and the other begins.

I drop my hand from her face, reaching down to pull her to her feet. "I'll take over your training myself." Darrold clears his throat, and I turn my head to glare at him. "Do you have something to say?"

His gaze shoots between me, Adara, and Jaz before coming back to me. "I only thought you'd be busy with... um." He rubs the back of his neck, my eyes narrowing into slits. "Maybe Jaz could train with you too. She's already ahead of the rest of the kids here."

Jaz, holding Adara's other hand, jumps up and down. "Can I? Please!" Sensing my hesitation, she juts out her lip in a pout. "Please!"

Adara's hand tightens in mine, and a sharp burst of panic floods me—her panic. I rub the back of her hand with my thumb, relishing in the mate bond flowing between us again. "Fine. But only half the time. The other half you'll be coming here. I can't spend all my time babysitting."

Jaz pumps her fist into the air, oblivious to Adara's fear. But is she afraid of me? Or her powers?

---

"Again," I say, staring down at Adara where she sits slumped on the ground, trying to catch her breath.

"Gideon, I—"

"Again," I snap.

"You can do it," Jaz says, smiling down at her and reaching out a hand.

Groaning in frustration, she lets the girl pull her to her feet, and I hold back the wolf trying to rush forward, wanting to be the one to help her. "Fine." Adara's mouth twists into a snarl as she stares at me for a moment, closing her eyes just as silver floods them.

"Start from the beginning. Reach out—"

"I know that," she sighs. "It just isn't working."

"It's never going to work if you don't actually believe it will," Jaz says, trying to encourage her, but I can feel Adara's frustration growing.

"Get out of your own way, little witch." I smirk when her eyes crack open to throw daggers at me. I know she hates the nickname, but that makes it all the more fun.

Huffing, she throws up her arms. "It isn't working. She won't let me grab her. She... It just isn't working." She drops back down to the ground, laying back and staring at the cloudy sky above. Her dark hair fans out around her, contrasting with the sharp green grass.

It's been a couple of days of training in the back yard, and we haven't made any progress outside of being able to pull her claws out without fully shifting. But she still can't shift at will unless provoked. Jaz, though, is making incredible progress.

"That's enough for today," I say, glancing between them. "Jaz, Madrona is waiting in the driveway to take you home."

She opens her mouth to protest, but glancing at Adara, she closes it quickly, nodding. "See you next week?"

Adara rolls her head toward her with a small smile. "Yeah, see you then."

Jaz's face lights up, and she skips to the front yard. A few minutes later, gravel crunches under

Madrona's tires as she cruises down the driveway. I move to sit down beside Adara in the grass, unable to resist the temptation of running my fingers through her hair.

"Why did you agree to let Jaz train with us?" she asks, her voice soft.

"Because she could use the challenge. And you could use the friend."

She turns her face toward me, worry etched into her face. "But what if I hurt her?"

I stop toying with the silky strand of black hair in my hand and look at her. "Did you hurt her when you lost control before?" I already know the answer, but I raise my brows until she shakes her head. "Then, why would you hurt her as you learn control now? You may not know how to control your powers, *yet*, but your magic, like your wolf, stems from who you are inside. You don't want to hurt Jaz, so you didn't." Reaching out, I stroke a finger down her cheek, caressing the frown of her lips. "*Mia fiamma*, you have to learn to trust yourself. If you keep holding yourself back out of fear, you'll never learn your full strength. Or control."

She twists toward me, her brows furrowed and her eyes searching mine. "Tell me why you say that. What does that mean? And don't give me some bullshit answer this time. What's with the nickname?"

I chuckle, remembering the kitchen when she asked me the same question as I walked out. I could feel her irritation as I climbed the stairs, and even during the drive to Darrold's. I grab her wrists, pulling her on top of me as I lay back. Her hair falls forward, curtaining around us, and I cup the back of her neck to hold her close to me. Her breath on my lips drives my wolf to the edge, but I shove him back—barely. "You want to know what it means? The nickname you insist is an insult?" My gaze dips to her parted lips. "And what if it is?"

Anger flares in her eyes. She pulls back, but I tighten my hold on her neck, my other hand gripping her hip, pinning her to me.

"What if it isn't?" I whisper, just before I crush my lips to hers, drowning in the taste of her. I suck her bottom lip into my mouth and nip it, a tiny drop of blood entering my mouth as I pull a moan from her. A growl escapes me because it's the same as the first time—the first drink of water after being lost in a drought. This witch tastes like bliss.

Her hands fist my shirt, and I press my tongue to the seam of her lips. She grants my entrance easily, parting her mouth as I thrust my tongue inside. I'll never get enough of her. My witch. My mate. My personal addiction.

She shoves off me, moving back to sit on the ground, a hand pressed to her lips. Silver dominates her irises, and her chest rises and falls rapidly. "I..."

"Tell me why you can't control your magic." My voice comes out hoarse, desire coursing through me, but she won't stay here with me if she keeps thinking about that kiss—her desire mixing with my own inside me. And I can't stop touching her if I keep thinking about the way she tastes.

She blinks a few times, tucking hair behind her ear and chewing on her lower lip. "Um, well, I... never had much magic."

I nod, remembering this, trying to avoid staring at her working her lip. "Yes, you told me that."

"Well, every time I cast even a small spell, I'd get it almost right, burning or melting a coffee pot or setting off a breaker in the house." She shrugs, her mouth pulled down into a frown as she stares down at her hands. "Then, Monique trapped me there. I-I knew she'd kill me. She'd kill everyone." She glances up at me, her cheeks flaming. "She'd kill you," she adds softly.

"That was the first time you used that much magic?"

She nods, avoiding my gaze. "Successfully anyway."

"I know the basics of witches' abilities. Spells and charms," I hold up one finger, "necromancy, though that's outlawed after the whole Salem Witch Trials," I add a finger. "Then, your prized oracles," I add a third finger and roll my eyes. "And leeches, rare as they are. It makes you wonder if they're rare because they could steal *anyone's* powers. It's quite a coincidence. However," I look up at her, fighting to keep my eyes from drifting down her body, "I have yet to hear of fire."

Adara takes a deep breath. "Well, there's archaic magic, which is elemental. Water, earth, air, and fire—the rarest. No one has been born with archaic magic in at least half a century, but fire archaic magic has been closer to three or four centuries now, I think." She shrugs. "I wouldn't even know who to ask in my coven about this power, let alone know how to learn control of it."

"Did you ever stop to think that when you cast a spell in the past, it wasn't you but the magic you were forcing?"

Her eyes snap to mine, and I put my hands out to her, palms up, waiting until she decides to rest her hands in mine.

"What if the coffee pot melted because you cast a spell? But your magic is fire. Fire melts, doesn't it?" I curl my fingers around hers, feeling the warmth of her skin beneath my touch. "What if you've had it all along?"

"Stop," she whispers, pulling her hands back.

My skin goes cold without her touch, and I frown at her. "Stop what? Training you? Or talking in general? Because I—"

"You can't just talk like I've always been powerful when we both know the truth." Gathering to her feet, she stomps over to the sliding door and shoves it open.

Irritated, I follow after her, Kaylus rustling in the branches above us. He stills when I glower at him before stepping into the house. "What the hell does that even mean?"

She whirls around, shoving her finger into my chest. "It means no one wants a powerless witch who can't control her wolf for a mate. Isn't that what you told me? We know what I am. That's exactly why I can't get this training right. Because I'm *not* strong. I'm *not* powerful. I'm weak, and I'm a danger to everyone here." She throws her hands in the air, her voice rising with each sentence. "Look around you! You're supposed to be the alpha of this pack, but you've spent half your week babysitting me instead. What are you going to do if I get one of you killed? What kind of alpha does that make you?" Hot tears stream down her face, and she turns to rush upstairs.

I reach out and grab her wrist, spinning her around and holding her against my chest. Sobs wrack her body, her shoulders shaking, and a lump forms in my own throat at her pain. "You will be the most powerful lycan witch there is. Because I believe it, even if you don't." I brush a hand down her hair, tucking it behind her ear and tipping her face up to me with my finger hooked under her chin. "Until you believe in yourself, you'll never master your wolf or your flames, so believe in me, *mia fiamma*, my flame, because I've been alive for centuries, and I've never seen anything like you in my lifetime. I've never believed anything more strongly." Softly, I press my lips to hers in a quick kiss, but she pulls away.

"But what if I hurt you? Or your pack? What—"

I lay my forehead against hers, tightening my arms around her. "Darling, we both know exactly who you are, and I would love to watch the world burn into ashes at your feet. Hell, I'd give you the lit match if you ever needed it. But we both know you'd lay flames only to protect those you love."

She takes a shaky breath, and I smile, placing a kiss on her forehead before loosening my hold.

"Go shower and check in with your raven. I'll get dinner started." I watch her climb the stairs, waiting until I hear her door click shut to reach for the nearest anything—a glass vase—and hurl it at the wall. The glass shatters, showering down into a thousand shards on the floor. I'll kill that witch who raised her—who snuffed her out into this tiny burning ember that feels alone and worthless. I'll kill the whole coven just to make them pay for the way she's suffered all these years because no one—*no one*—gets to hurt her and lives to talk about it.

## CHAPTER SEVEN
### *Adara*

I JUMP WHEN I HEAR THE GLASS SHATTER downstairs, Gideon's rage pulsing through me distantly. I lick my lips, pushing the urge to rush downstairs to him away, and grab the silver communicator.

*Any updates?*

Jules texts back almost immediately. *Yes, but it's not good.*

I rub a hand over my forehead, running my fingers through my hair. *What is it?*

*Mom's loyalty was questioned at a coven meeting. She volunteered to lead the hunt.*

"Shit," I mutter under my breath.

*I want to stay with you, Addy. Please.*

*No,* I send. *You have to stay there. Safe and hidden. Chloe will help you. Keep me updated. Love you.*

*Addy...*

I blink back my tears, my heart aching to see Jules and know she's okay, to hear her laugh and see her smile. But knowing the coven sent out the bounty hunters is enough to keep me in hiding. They're ruthless and powerful... and I'm...

What am I?

*A stubborn princess?* my wolf offers.

Setting the communicator down with a scowl, I take in my hands, staring at my palms. Am I powerful? Kaylus swoops in through the window, landing in his nest, and I jump.

*"Well, that was a show. Is it your time of the month or something?"*

I swat at him, and he caws.

*"What? You were the one acting like your hormones were in control."*

I laugh despite myself. "I can't stand you."

*"You need me, and you know it."*

"I just don't know how to do all this." I wave my hand around the room, and he tilts his head. "Believe in myself. In Gideon. In *this*. He said that my spells before didn't work because my fire was too powerful, but that can't be it. Why wouldn't the coven have trained me for it?"

*"If Monique told them you were useless and had no power, they would've believed her without question, Addy."* He tilts his head the other way. *"They wouldn't have bothered testing you if she never told them. Plus, fire magic hasn't been seen in centuries. They would've thought it impossible."*

"Right. Of course she would do that," I scoff. "Just like she knows Jules is gifted but won't send her to the academy. How could I be so stupid and naive?" My fingers curl into fists, and all I want is to scream. She's taken so much from me, and now this too? All these lies, and they just keep building and building, growing until they teeter. I want to bury her beneath them and the carnage they'll reap. It's the least she deserves.

I hiss a breath as my nails lengthen into claws, piercing my palms slightly. Blood beads along the punctures, and I close my eyes, taking a deep breath. I reach out to my wolf, to the winter clearing from before, and find her lapping water from a small stream.

*You seem different,* she says, nonchalant at the changes she's fully aware of.

"I want you to teach me."

She lifts her head and looks back at me over her shoulder. *Teach you?*

"Yes," I whisper. "I don't want to control you. I want to learn."

Pride pours off the black wolf before me, and I can't help the smile that spreads across my face as I drop to my knees.

She pads forward and presses her forehead to mine, reminding me of Gideon when he held me just moments ago.

*First...*

The world spins around us, and I shut my eyes tightly, trying to swallow back the nausea and dizziness.

*Open your eyes, girl.*

My wolf's voice is commanding and stern, and the smell of patchouli fills my nose. My eyes snap open, knowing only one person who smells like that.

A young Monique paces across the floor of a penthouse apartment, the Boston Skyline framed by the large windows behind her. We must be in the high priestesses' Harbor apartment. I look around the space, furnished lavishly with lush carpet and simple yet delicate decor—paintings of misty forests, candles and crystals covering the tabletop. A stack of black tarot cards sits on the coffee table.

"Sit," Batya says, staring at Monique with her icy blue eyes. Her deep red hair is cut to her shoulders, and her long nails tap the deck again.

Monique reluctantly sits, glancing to the end of the couch where a small baby sleeps.

"What question do you seek?" Batya asks, shuffling the deck slowly.

"You already know why I came here." Monique sighs when the oracle pauses shuffling and narrows her gaze. "Alright, alright. I... came for my daughter. Something isn't right. Her fingers are so... hot." She chews on her bottom lip, staring over at the infant until Batya sets three cards down.

Batya closes her eyes, then flips over each card one at a time. The Moon. The Devil, but it's upside down. Strength. Brows furrowed, she pulls three more from the deck. Eight of cups. Ace of spheres. The Lovers.

"What is this?" Monique asks, glancing from the cards to Batya.

Batya sighs. "You have fears hidden inside you. You must cleanse yourself, be able to trust your intuition without clouding your judgment with dreams and imaginations."

"This isn't about me. I-it's about her." Monique points at the bundle, her finger trembling.

Batya glares at her. "Hush. The cards show you." Glancing at the set before her again, she continues. "There is a great struggle coming. The cycle will break. The chains must fall, and then great power will flourish. This change will bring what was missing, and the unpredicted pairing will fill the void. Together, they will create a new world." Frowning, she pulls one last card—the Tower—and gasps. "But catastrophe is looming on the horizon."

Fear shadows Monique's face, her shoulders tensing to her ears. "I have to go," she whispers, moving to scoop up the crying baby. "Shh, Adara, shhh," she coos impatiently, as she rushes out the door.

Batya watches her leave with curiosity, pulling a card off the top of the deck without looking. "The Fool," she muses, a smile breaking across her face. "How amusing. What we come as, we end as, but, oh, so much potential." She taps her chin with the card, looking at the still open door. "So much potential."

The room spins again, and I reach out, grasping my wolf's fur as I remember where we are. "What's happening? Why are we seeing this?"

*Shh. Watch.*

The kitchen of my childhood home materializes before me, and Monique stands watching from the doorway as a toddler wanders around the living room. She holds a phone to her ear, watching the younger me play with blocks.

"It's wearing off," she hisses into the phone. "Her power is growing *again*. She melted her pacifier yesterday!"

She runs a hand through her hair, pulling at the soft blonde curls.

"Can you please bring me another dose? I'll strengthen it with my own spell." A pause. "I *know* how dangerous it is. I didn't ask you for your *gods damn opinion*." She slams her hand against the wall, making me jump. "Just bring it. I have to suppress this power for good before she ruins everything!" She hangs up and throws the phone across the room, shattering a window in the kitchen and making the toddler scream.

Snapping my attention over, I see two wood blocks on fire in her tiny dimpled hands.

"Adara, no!" Monique snaps, and the vision fades.

The spinning doesn't affect me as badly when I'm thrown back into the snowy clearing. Tears threaten to spill down my face, and my wolf steps forward and rests her chin on my shoulder. I bury my face into her fur and cry—heavy, heart-aching sobs threatening to shatter me.

*I'm sorry... Do you understand now?*

Sniffling, I pull away and wipe the heel of my hand across my cheeks. "That my mother has hated me my entire life? Yeah, I got the picture pretty clearly."

My wolf huffs. *No, that you've always had power, so much that she's feared you since you were just an infant.*

Startled at her tone, I look away and blink back the rest of my tears. Revisiting the two visions, I know that it was obvious. But still, I mourn for the childhood I wish I'd had, the mother I needed. "I... I saw."

*Don't let her smother you any longer. Don't let her win. You have to remember the cards, girl. The Lovers. The Strength.*

My mouth goes dry, knowing she's talking about Gideon. The Lovers has always symbolized perfection in romance, balanced and compatible, the epitome of happiness and love. Soulmates.

*You have to believe in yourself. In me. In our power.* She nudges my shoulder with her snout. *We were meant to be, just as surely as we were destined to be mated with the alpha. Claim it.*

"I can't... I can't control it. The flames." I look at her, drowning in her silver depths as I verbalize the very thing I fear the most. "I'm going to hurt them." The pack. The ones who've accepted me. Jaz and Mila and Frank. And Jules. And Gideon.

The forest erupts into a forest fire, embers dancing in the air around us, the snow melting almost instantly. *Claim your wolf to claim your mate to claim your power. Her head tilts to one side as she gazes at me. Claim it all so the witches cannot.*

A hard knock startles me, and I shudder a gasp as I'm pulled from my mind and back into my body, in my bedroom, with Kaylus staring at me from his nest.

"Adara?" Gideon asks from the other side of the door.

I clear my throat, disheveled and still not showered.

"The door is locked. Let me in, or I'm breaking it open," he growls.

I jump off the bed and unlock the door, opening it wide to see him running his hands through his thick black hair.

"Gods, finally." He studies me from the hallway, his gaze traveling from my dry hair to my clothes. "You haven't showered."

It's a statement, not a question, and my cheeks heat when I realize I don't know how long I've been in here. "Uh, I..."

He laughs, the sound low and husky, making my mouth go dry. "Let's go." He turns, moving down the stairs, and I glance over my shoulder at Kaylus, sleeping beside the bed, before rushing after Gideon. He walks past the kitchen and out the sliding door into the yard.

"Wait, I thought we—"

"You look like you need some air," he says, throwing a look over his shoulder. He smirks and takes off into the woods. The sun has started its slow descent toward the horizon, but there's plenty of light left in the sky to see the pair of sweatpants Gideon tosses behind him before he shifts, giving me the briefest glimpse of toned thighs leading to his bare ass.

My wolf begs for release in my chest, and I pull my shirt over my head as I race after him. A smile breaks across my face as I shift painlessly and chase his black wolf through the shadows of the trees in the dying golden light.

## CHAPTER EIGHT
*Gideon*

ADARA CRASHES THROUGH THE FOREST AFTER me, and I relish in it—her wolf chasing mine through the woods. My wolf gloats inside my head, rubbing it in that he told me this was right, that I should've listened to him from the start.

*"What were you doing in your room?"* I ask her, trying to drown out the insufferable wolf inside me.

*"Bonding, I guess."*

I quirk a brow, ducking under some low branches and stomping through the brush. The setting sun lights the forest path in a fiery orange glow, the fallen leaves on the ground bright and mesmerizing.

*"Have you ever... visited your wolf?"* she asks, hesitation clear in her tone.

I slow my pace, and she stumbles as she catches up to me. *"Twice."* After meeting my first alpha, when I first learned of the supernatural world, my wolf dragged into his realm—all obsidian mountains and a field of the strangest flowers I'd ever seen... asphodels, he called them. The second time was when I shut him out of my mind, closing off his world and his access to the rest of me... until I met her.

Her eyes snap over to me. *"Just twice? Is... is it unusual to go more than that?"*

I shrug, inhaling the fresh scent of the lake as we near. *"It's different for everyone. Some never enter the realm of their wolf. Some enter it frequently."* Padding through the tree line, we break into the field with the lake, and I nip her shoulder, then run off.

She laughs, the sound like a breath of fresh air on the first spring morning after a harsh winter. Jumping on my back, she tackles me to the ground, and I roll beneath her. Her teeth graze my snout, and I turn to pin her down. She wiggles beneath me as I lay on top of her, and I run my nose along her cheek.

*"Bet you can't catch me."* I bolt off her and crash into the lake, diving under the water and shifting beneath the surface. I swim a few strokes, still amazed at the water. I've been visiting this lake for so long, but it never freezes, the temperature always staying chilly, even in the height of summer, yet never dropping so low that ice would form on its surface.

At first, I thought it was a witch's territory, but after researching all the covens in the country, I've found none anywhere near this lake. Adara's coven is the nearest in the area, and they're based closer to the city limits. Only Monique lived as far from the city as she did, most likely to hide her two daughters and their true abilities.

Thinking of her puts a sour taste in my mouth, and I clench my jaw, shooting up to break the surface of the lake. Panting, I look around for Adara, but there's no sign of her. The ripples along the water's surface all come from my direction, and there's no signs of movement in the field. "Adara?" I call out, treading water to stay afloat as I spin myself in circles looking for her. "Adara!"

A hand wraps around my ankle, and I'm pulled under water before I can take a full breath of air into my lungs. I lurch up, swimming toward the surface as my chest burns, and the fingers around my ankle heat the water around me. Adara's hands climb up my body, her legs wrapping around my waist, her mouth covering mine. She smiles against my lips as we push to the surface, both of us trying to catch our breath.

"Caught you," she says, bursting into a breathless laugh.

"I've no idea how," I say, smiling at the joy on her face. "Still a brat."

She splashes water at me, then moves to swim away, but I grab her wrist and pull her back to me. An arm wrapped around her waist, I crush her chest to mine. My eyes search hers, her slightly parted lips, her lashes darkened with water, her flushed cheeks. Bending my head down, I press my lips to hers before sucking her bottom one into my mouth and nipping slightly.

"How did you catch me?" I whisper, my narrowed gaze taking in her sudden smirk.

"Wouldn't you like to know." She tries to swim away again, laughing when I pull her back to me.

"Come on, little witch." I tilt her jaw up with a finger crooked beneath her chin, trailing kisses from her lips to her jaw. "Tell me your secrets," I say, kissing down her neck into the dip of her collarbone.

She swallows hard, and her hands come up to cling onto my shoulders.

"How did you pull me beneath the water?" I nip at her shoulder, then slide my tongue over the reddened skin, smirking as she shivers beneath my touch.

"My wolf," she breathes.

I pull my head back, my brows furrowed. "Your wolf? Did you tap into the mate bond?"

She nods, her eyes wide with surprise. "Did I do it wrong? Did I hurt you? Gods, I—"

"No, no, you didn't hurt me. I'm just surprised." I lean my forehead against hers. "You'd have to be very bonded with your wolf to tap into my strength. I... I haven't even tried it myself." I rub the tip of my nose against hers. "You are as unpredictable as a flame, *mia fiamma*. And just as fierce."

She smiles when I kiss her forehead. "If I'm the flame, what does that make you?"

I chuckle. "The trees, of course."

She scrunches up her face. "No—"

"Yes. You consume me, and I will happily feed your fire as you reduce this world to ash."

She pulls away sharply, tearing herself from my arms and swimming to shore. "Why do you keep talking like that? I don't *want* to destroy everything, Gideon!"

I swim behind her, following her to the shoreline where the grass meets the water's edge. "Fire doesn't just destroy. It cleanses. Adara," I reach out, entwining her fingers with mine. "Fire allows new life to grow, new beginnings to flourish. Flames burn the old to ash, and the earth recaptures that into its soil to breathe new life into the world."

Staring down at our hands, she sighs. "I'm tired. I think I'll head back and go to bed."

"Let's go then." I squeeze her hand, but she shakes her head.

"I'd like the time to think. You stay," she says.

Frowning, I duck my head to catch her gaze.

She gives me a small smile. "I'll be fine." Rising onto her tiptoes, she places a gentle kiss on my cheek and turns to leave, shifting as she moves toward the trees.

Watching until she disappears into the woods, I sigh, then turn toward the water. Sliding back in, I make a few laps to work off the frustration of knowing I somehow pissed her off again, or at the very least pushed her away.

*You're growing clingy*, my wolf laughs.

"Go away," I growl, wading through the water toward the grassy shore.

"You won't even hear me out?" a small voice asks.

My head whips around, finding Aramin standing by the tree line, her arms wrapped around her naked body. Dirt covers most of her skin, and leaves are woven through her matted hair. Her minty scent clings to her, hidden beneath another layer of... something foul. My lip curls in disgust. "No, go back to whatever shithole you crawled out of." I make my way toward the tree line, wanting to swing by the house before I head to the bar, knowing I need to check on how things are going there but that I won't be able to focus until I know Adara is alright.

Aramin's arms wrap tighter around her middle, her eyes focused on the ground at my feet. "Please, Dee. I didn't meant to hurt you—"

A harsh laugh escapes me, and I turn back to her. "Wasn't that exactly your intention? Take your bullshit lies and *leave*, Aramin. You have no business here."

Her eyes snap to mine, anger raging behind their mossy green color. "I didn't tell the council you were mates, even though it was ridiculously obvious."

I narrow my gaze at her. "And why is that? Why did you leave that part out?"

Her jaw clenches, and she takes a deep breath through her nose. "Because I didn't want to hurt *you*.

Just her." She steps forward, standing before me with softened eyes. "I knew you'd be fine. Even if you got in trouble, they'd never hurt you." Her hand reaches up to touch my cheek, a gentle smile on her lips, and I snatch her wrist with a snarl, making her eyes widen.

"Don't ever touch me," I growl, my gaze flicking between her eyes. "Leave. Now."

Her temper flares, and she narrows her eyes at me, leaning in to close the small gap between us.

My wolf snarls inside, recoiling away from the way her skin touches ours. It's wrong—disgusting, unwanted, like a sweater of wool and pine needles that fell into swamp water.

Her breath is hot against my lips when she speaks, her glare boring into me. "This isn't pack territory, *Dee*. You'll do well to remember that when you sneak here with that bitch of yours." Backing away, she holds my gaze, a malicious smirk splitting her face. "Watch your back. You aren't the only alpha around here."

Then, she shifts in an instant, her red fur dissolving into the shadows of the darkening woods.

My jaw ticks as I work to keep my wolf at bay. Chasing her is exactly what she wants me to do, lead me into whatever trap she's set out for me.

*Not if you kill her first*, my wolf argues.

"Not worth it." I turn in the opposite direction, needing to see Adara safe at home. I make a mental note to call Mila to hang out with her while I go to the bar too. I don't want her alone after this.

*Don't grow weak on me, Gideon.*

"We'll hunt in time, but it'll be on my terms, on my time. Not hers." What the hell is Aramin up to? I'm not the only alpha around here, and my lake isn't pack territory? She's delusional. This lake has been in my pack territory since I claimed these woods. I may not be the only alpha in New England, but I'm the strongest. She's a fool to think anyone could overthrow me.

*Best to be cautious*, he warns.

Growling, I shove his voice away. Anyone who dares to challenge me and threaten my mate can enjoy a slow death at my hands.

Slamming through the bar doors, I storm through the crowd toward my office door. I don't slow my pace to allow Adara to keep up with me, and she enters through the doors a moment behind me, her glare burning into my back. Frank looks up from his full bar, glancing between us. He reaches under the bar and grabs a bottle of whiskey, holding it over the bar top out to me as I pass. I snatch it from his hand and shove the door shut behind me, muting the noise of the crowded bar behind the thick wood door.

Grumbling to myself, I slump into my chair and drink straight from the bottle. After the lake, I checked on Adara, as planned, but instead of Mila coming to stay with her, Adara insisted on coming here.

*"I still need to make money for my sister, Gideon, and you can't just keep me in this house like a prisoner."* She put her hands on her hips and stared at me from the kitchen doorway as I sat on one of the island stools.

*"I really don't want you at the bar working like that."* I sighed and rubbed a hand over my face.

*"Why?"* She walked forward and grabbed my hand. *"Wouldn't it make more sense to keep me near you?"*

*I looked up at her, knowing she had a point. "But my mate shouldn't be working in my bar like some low level employee."*

*"I'm not a low level employee."* She smirked, shrugging. *"You aren't the boss of me, so when we go, I'll be doing what I want."*

Godsforsaken witch—she's more insufferable than any woman I've ever met. I gulp down more of the whiskey before setting the bottle on the desk and pulling my notebooks toward me. Frowning at the office door for a moment, I try to brush away the gnawing feeling in my gut that although I like having her here, I hate having her so far from me, on the other side of the door. But she'll never agree to just sit here, not when she's so worried about making enough money for her sister.

A sudden smile breaks across my face as the problem essentially solves itself.

Balancing the books takes longer than usual after having taken a few days off for the council and settling Adara in. I blow out a breath as I lean back in my chair, glad to be done with the most boring part of my life here, though there's a slight comfort in the monotony and consistency numbers provide. A light tapping on the window steals my attention, and I slowly drag myself over to open it.

The night air is stale, suffocating without the usual chilly breeze cutting through it. The hair on the back of my neck stands, and my wolf paces inside my chest. Something isn't right...

I start to shove the window closed, then notice a small package sitting on the ground outside, just beyond the window frame. Reaching down, I hook a finger through the string holding the brown paper together and lift it inside. It's light and small, the size of my palm. I use a lengthened claw to slice the tie off, unfolding the paper to reveal a thick white note.

You're running out of time, Disantollo. - A

I lift up the note, a smooth glossy texture on the back. Flipping it over, I see a photo of Adara sitting in Darrold's back yard on the first day she trained with him. Looking at the note again, the initial catches my eye, and rage coils in my gut. The metallic tang of blood coats my mouth as I clench my jaw so hard my fangs pierce into my lip.

I throw the paper onto my desk, lunging at the window, but the air is alive with movement, the breeze cold and fresh, no hint of mint lingering in its wake. Growling, I slam and lock the window before throwing open the office door. "Frank!"

His head snaps in my direction, and he gives an imperceptible nod. Smiling as the picture of calm, he sets two full beers on the bar in front of two of our regulars before stepping out from behind it in my direction. "What happened?" he asks, his voice low.

I rake my eyes across the dimly lit bar, smoke hazing around the crowd. I spot Adara easily, her black hair pulled up into a ponytail high on her head. She smiles at her table, four women sipping beers and laughing at whatever she said. "My desk. Someone dropped a *love note* outside my window." Curling my hands into fists, I cross my arms over my chest. I stay in the bar, hidden in the shadows beside the open door, my eyes glued to the dark-haired witch walking amongst my wolves as Frank walks into my office.

"Who's it from?" he asks when he returns to my side.

"Who do you think?" I scowl at the crowd. "Aramin visited me earlier today, warned me that I'm not the *only alpha around*."

Frank shakes his head. "Was that before or after she tried to stake a claim?"

"Rejection never looked good on her."

He laughs, but it's void of his usual mirth. "Now what?"

"Put out a pack alert—only to the hunters for now. If Aramin is spotted, she's brought to me. I want to know what her game is."

He presses his lips together, stroking his beard with one hand. "Detain? Not eliminate?"

"I don't believe she's working alone," I growl.

Raising his brows, he turns to face me. "Who would join a suicide mission against you? You aren't thinking Kilch would be this stupid?"

"That's exactly what I want to figure out."

"He's all bark, boss. I doubt he has enough balls to bite, especially against you."

Scoffing, I shove off the wall, making my way to Adara and pulling her into my arms. "We're leaving," I whisper into her ear.

She quirks a brow at me. "I have tables—"

"I don't care." I lift her into my arms, walking from the bar and setting her in the passenger seat of my truck.

"Gideon," she glowers at me.

"Not now." I climb into the cab and start the engine, peeling out of the parking lot and driving home, staring straight ahead at the road and ignoring the questions I know are on the tip of her tongue. But I can't deal with those right now because if I focus on anything other than getting her back to the house in one piece, anything other than the woman sitting in the seat beside me and keeping her safe, I'll force Kilch's hand and make him regret ever running his mouth. You can't talk up an alpha challenge without waking the beast, and if anyone should know that, it's him.

## CHAPTER NINE
### Adara

GIDEON'S KNUCKLES TURN WHITE AS HE GRIPS the steering wheel, his eyes searing through the windshield at the road before us. "What happened?" I ask after a few minutes of silence, unable to hold back my questions any longer.

He scoffs, his jaw ticking as he runs a hand through his hair.

"Don't ignore me. You just ripped me away from four tables at the start of a good night. I could've—"

"I don't care how much money you could've made, Adara," he says, his voice low and full of authority. "I don't care how many tables you had or how shitty it was of me to rip you out of there. I don't care about any of that. So, just sit there, let me take you home, and for once in your life, be quiet."

Every other question lingering on my tongue dies in my throat. It takes every ounce of control to keep my wolf inside through the anger and frustration coursing through me. A voice in the back of my head suggests being patient, that he must have some reason for doing what he's doing, but I don't want to be patient right now. I want to be angry.

Pulling me out of the bar means I just lost all the tips I was making, and could've kept making. It means I'm set back from paying Jules's tuition—again. Because first, I lost the money in the bar when Gideon bit me, then Monique found my totes.

The truck pulls into the driveway, and I throw the door open before he puts it in park.

"Adara," he calls after me, but I'm halfway through the front door.

I don't stop, walking straight through the back door into the yard, aiming for the tree line. My wolf itches to get out, to shake out her fur, to chase the moon where it sits high in the sky. We need to run, to breathe, to get some space before we do exactly what Gideon always says we will—burn everything to ashes.

*"Addy?"* Kaylus's voice is filled with concern, as he flies from the treetops onto a lower branch. *"What's wrong?"*

"Adara!" Gideon storms through the backdoor and into the yard, grabbing my arm and spinning me to face him. "What the hell are you doing?"

"Me?" I scream, shoving him with both hands. "What am *I* doing? I don't know, I guess it depends what I'm allowed to do as your prisoner!"

"I'm only trying to keep you safe." He grabs both my wrists, holding me in place when I try to pull away. "Gods above, you make it almost impossible! It's like you *want* to be killed!"

A lump forms in my throat, and tears blur my vision. "Well, you'd all be better off if I were, so why don't you just let me go?" I try to pull away again, struggling against his hold. "Damn it, Gideon, just let me go!"

He sucks a breath through his teeth, glancing down where his hands touch my skin, but he refuses to let go. "No," he says through clenched teeth. "I won't let you. Not now, not ever." He pulls me closer, guiding my hands behind his back until I'm pressed against his chest. "I won't let anyone touch you. Not the council, not your coven, not your homicidal mother. No one will touch you because I won't let them. You can burn me," he leans forward, his lips brushing against mine, "you can scream at me, you can bite me, but I'll never leave you to fight alone." Dipping his head, his lips capture mine, claiming me. He licks along the seam of my lips, and I open, granting him entrance as his tongue strokes mine.

Something snaps inside me, and when his hands let go of my wrists, I clutch at his back, fisting his shirt to press his body harder to mine. Because I need him—all of him. He moves to bury his hands in my hair, hissing at the contact, and I break the kiss. Pulling my head back, I search his face and turn my head when he tries to kiss me again, grabbing his hand and flipping it over. Blisters form along his palm and fingers—swollen, dark red burns cover from wrist to fingertips. I look up into his eyes, tears dripping down my cheeks. "I-I did this. I *hurt* you." I let him go, dropping his hand as if he burned me and not the other way around.

He reaches for me as I step away, but I brush him off. "Adara, stop. It's fine. It just takes a bit longer to heal because it's—"

"Because it's fire magic," I whisper. "I know that. I know what I am and the danger I pose to you. This is why I needed to train and get control. This is why I can't be here. I can't be with you!"

"Your powers are growing faster than I thought they would." He shoves his hands behind his back, hiding the burns, but it's too late—I already know they exist. "We can train more to make up for it."

"How can you be this calm? After everything, losing your family, and now you're sitting here protecting me when I possess the one magic that should scare you." Swiping away the tears running down my cheeks, I shove my wolf away as she whispers to me that it's because he loves me. Because how could he love me when I'm a walking reminder of all the pain and loss he's suffered?

His face twists at my words, pain flitting across his face. "You didn't kill my family, *mia fiamma*, and you can think every horrible thing about yourself that you want, but I know you'd never do such a horrible thing to anyone, no matter what kind of magic you have."

Stepping toward me, he reaches out his hand, palm down. "Come on, let's—"

I step back, afraid to touch him. "No... I'm just... I'm going to bed." I turn and run into the house, rushing up the stairs and locking the bedroom door behind me. Tears pour down my cheeks, and I put a hand over my mouth to muffle my sobs. Kaylus swoops in through the window, landing on his nest and gazing at me.

*"Addy... it was just an accident..."*

I stumble to the bed, burrowing under the covers, and he hops over to me, resting his beak on my head as I cry myself to sleep.

*Tall pines tower above me as I lay on the cool dirt floor. Bare branches of maples and oaks create an eerie canopy above me, blotting out the light of the full moon. I struggle to my feet, putting a hand to my head as the world spins around me. It's so dark in these woods, and that smell... ashy and blackened, like the earth after a forest fire.*

*My mouth goes dry as I recognize that scent—Lockwood Forest. My grandmother's words rush back to me, "If evil lurks within its walls, doom will fall upon us all." I shiver as her gold eyes flash in my mind, filled with warning.*

*I take a few steps toward one of the many paths leading out of the small clearing I landed in, waiting for the dark magic to throw me back into my bed. Passing outside the boundaries of the clearing, I reach a path and look around. This is the farthest I've ever gotten before. I glance behind me, wondering if I should be on a different path.*

No, this one, *my wolf's voice says, and I turn forward again.*

*Nodding, I agree with her. This one just feels right.*

*I travel down the path slowly, searching for any signs of the witch that haunts this forest and guards the well. Her magic smells dark and uninviting, and it makes my skin crawl with a thousand spiders the farther I go.*

*"How did you get here?" a woman's voice hisses.*

*I whirl around, searching the woods around me, but it's dark—too dark to see but a few feet in front of me. "Who are you?"*

*"You come into my den and demand answers," she says, her voice echoing around me.*

Behind you, *my wolf warns.*

*I spin, ducking my head as something whooshes over me, and I reach out, grabbing the woman's leg. Pulling, I rip her off balance and pin her to the forest floor. "Who are you?" I demand slowly, leaning closer, but her features swim before me, shadows clinging to her and concealing her identity.*

*"Who are you, lycan witch?" she spits. "How do you walk amongst others with that stench?"*

*My wolf rages inside me, and I wrestle with the witch on the ground, grabbing her wrists and crushing them beneath my knees.* "Answer me!"

She howls in pain and bucks her hips, rolling me to the side, but I don't let her go until claws pierce into the back of my hands.

A cry tears from me, and I release her, cradling both hands to my chest. The forest swirls around me, the scent shifting with the trees. Cedarwood, patchouli, and smoke invade my senses, and I struggle to my feet, stumbling forward as I follow the strange mixture. Fog grows thicker around me, and the dark night sky is moonless, leaving me with no light in the forest. A man screams, then a wolf howls, and a female's cackle of laughter stops me dead in my tracks.

Monique's laughter fades. "Where is she? Is that pathetic little witch still worth hiding here?"

No, no, no. I force my feet forward, tripping over loose rocks and roots on the ground. Coming through the tree line, I find myself in Gideon's back yard. My eyes frantically search the space, finding the blonde witch of my nightmares towering over a black wolf lying on the ground. Blood pools around him, and he whimpers weakly as her boot crushes his paw into the dirt.

"No!" I scream, running forward and shoving her off him. I bury my face in his fur, listening to his heartbeat, slow but steady. Turning my head toward her, the brief relief I felt is quickly replaced with a raging ire.

"Finally, Adara. It's time to come home. Stop playing house with the dirty mutts and fulfill your duty to your coven." She raises her chin, looking down her nose at me. Disapproval and animosity drip off her, threatening to drown me in the ocean of hatred she's always harbored toward me.

"No," I growl.

She narrows her gaze. "Speak. Up. You know I hate your mumbling."

"No, I won't go anywhere with you!" I lunge at her, taking her by surprise as I tackle her to the ground.

She twists beneath me, muttering a spell under her breath.

"You don't get to hold power over me any longer," I say, grabbing the back of her head. I scream, moving to slam her face into the ground as fire lights up the grass around us.

But my scream doesn't stop, and a sharp pain throbs against my forehead.

Peck. Peck.

"Addy, wake up!"

Blinking the sleep from my eyes, I see Kaylus flying above me, and I bolt up. Dark smoke fills the air around me, and he caws.

"It's the bed," he says.

"Go, get out of here!" I swat at him, pushing him toward the open window frantically, unwilling to let another bear the marks of my uncontrolled flames. Looking around me, I survey the room and realize it's only the bed that's on fire. "How the hell do I put it out?" Coughing on the smoke, I move into the hallway, closing the door behind me, and gasp as my eye catches the sight of my hand on the doorknob.

Deep gashes cover the back of my hand, and I quickly glance at the other one, noticing the same pattern.

Claw marks.

My mouth goes dry as I pull each one closer to my face, inspecting the wounds that happened in a dream, yet exist in reality. The faint scent of palo santo fills my nostrils as I inspect the wounds slowly healing over. It's the dark magic of the Lockwood witch. My heart hammers in my chest, pounding against my ribcage as my mind struggles to piece everything together.

The dream, the clearing, the fight on the forest path—all of that was real. But... if that was real, then was the part with Monique real too?

My eyes snap to the hallway, looking in the direction of Gideon's room.

*He's safe.*

My wolf's words bring a small sense of relief knowing he's safe... for now.

Leaning against it back against the door, my hands fist my hair as I try to think of what to do, panicking when I realize I have no earthly idea—for the fire consuming my bed, the dark magic causing wounds that happen in my dreams to follow me into reality, or the fact that Monique killing Gideon feels more like a premonition than just a dream.

I take a deep breath, trying to steady my racing heart. The bed is the most immediate issue, but that still doesn't make it easy to figure out. I've been so focused on trying to control my fire magic, I never realized I should ask how to put it out.

*It has to consume what it's burning, then it will be done.*

My wolf's voice is comforting, but I groan inwardly when I realize I won't have anywhere to sleep after it's done. I slide down the door to the floor, resting my head on my knees, wishing more than anything that things could just be easy for once.

"I thought you said you'd help me control this," I grumble. "Now, Gideon's hands are wickedly blistered and my bed is literally burning to ash. Gideon was wrong. My intentions have nothing to do with my magic when I never wanted any of this to happen." Sighing, I tilt my head back against the door and close my eyes. "You can't control the fire any more than I can, can you?"

For once, my wolf is frustratingly quiet.

## CHAPTER TEN
*Gideon*

THE SCENT OF SMOKE SWIRLS AROUND ME, rousing me from my sleep. I untangle the sheets from around my legs and cross my bedroom in one step, flying into the hall. My breathing comes out in quick pants, and my heart rate slows only slightly when I see Adara leaning back against her door, little ribbons of smoke slipping from beneath the wood.

"What are you doing? We need to—"

Her eyes snap open, and she shoves her hands into her lap.

The words of needing a fire extinguisher die on my tongue. "What's on fire?"

She avoids my gaze, looking down at the ground. Misery covers her, the thick emotion oozing around her.

"Adara." I kneel down in front of her, cupping her cheek and raising her chin until I can look into her eyes.

She turns her face, ripping free of my grasp. Tears drip down her cheeks, and she presses farther against the door.

"Please," I say. "What happened? Is it safe to stay inside?"

A humorless huff of laughter quietly escapes her. "It's safe enough, I guess," she whispers.

Reaching out, I brush my thumb across her cheek, swiping away her tears. My heart clenches painfully at the sight of her. "What happened, little witch?"

She takes a shaky breath, her lips trembling. Her voice comes out as a hoarse whisper, and I strain to hear the words. "I set my bed on fire in my sleep."

"The... bed? Only that?" My brows furrow. "Is Kaylus—"

"He's fine. I shoved him out the window. But I... I can't put the flames out." She stares down at the floor, resting her forehead atop her knees as she pulls them tightly to her chest.

Settling beside her on the floor, I drape one arm over her shoulders, feeling her tense beneath my touch. "I have other places you can sleep, *mia fiamma*."

"I'll just burn them down," she says, defeated. "I'm not safe here—not for you or your house. Gods, Gideon." She scoots away from me, but I pull her back.

"The bed will be the only thing to burn?"

She nods slightly, keeping her head on her knees.

I slide my free hand under her knees, sliding the arm draped over her shoulders down her back for support. She yelps, grappling for a hold on my arm.

But I freeze, standing there in the smoke-filled hall with her in my arms, as I stare down at her hands.

Her eyes slowly follow my gaze, and she quickly tucks her hands away, out of sight.

"What happened, Adara?" I growl, fighting to keep my claws from coming out. My head snaps toward her door. "Is that why your bed is on fire? Did someone come—"

"N-no," she says. "No one is in there, I swear. I-I just had a bad dream."

My eyes narrow at her. "A dream gave you those wounds? A dream set your magic on edge enough to set the bed on fire?"

Her tongue darts out to lick her lips, and she nods almost imperceptibly.

"What. Dream?"

"Um..." She avoids my gaze, eyes darting around.

"Adara," I growl.

"It... I..." She licks her lips again. "It was my mother."

I clench my jaw so hard my teeth ache, inhaling a sharp breath through my nose before blowing it out as a deep sigh. "I want details, but... not tonight." My grip around her tightens, holding her against my chest, focusing on the weight of her in my arms as I make my way toward my room. A part of me never wants to put her down.

"W-what're you doing?"

"Taking you to bed. Yours is gone, and I'm not much for sleeping on the floor." I ignore the shocked look on her face, walking through the open door of my room and kicking it shut behind me. I drop her gently onto the bed and slide in next to her, pulling the covers over us both. My arm snakes around her waist and holds her to me, her back tight against my chest.

"I can't," she says, breathless.

"Where else would you sleep?" I whisper in her ear, pressing a kiss just behind it.

"I..." She swallows hard. "The couch."

"Mm, sorry, but the couch isn't available." I trail kisses down her neck and across her shoulder.

"W-why?"

Another kiss, my teeth grazing the soft curve of her neck. "Because I said it wasn't. This is the only other bed in my house. And if you find another option, I'll happily set it aflame myself."

Her breath hitches as I bite the lobe of her ear.

"I won't touch you any more than I am right now unless you tell me to," I breathe against her flushed skin. Gods, do I want her to tell me to.

She turns her face slightly to look at me, her pupils dilated. The salty scent of tears clings to her still, and I kiss her cheek, then her jaw. She sucks her lower lip into her mouth, her teeth pressing into the soft skin.

I kiss her softly once on her temple, then settle down beside her, keeping my arm around her waist.

"Sleep, *mia fiamma*. Tonight is not the night for decisions."

*Because whatever decisions she has to make don't include what you want.*

Closing my eyes, I shove my wolf and my worries away, focusing only on the warm body of my mate in my arms, in my bed. I wait to drift off to sleep until I feel her breathing even out, light snores escape her as exhaustion wins whatever battle is going on inside her. Then, finally, sleep takes me as well.

Inhaling deeply, the light forest scent that clings to Adara fills my lungs. Woodsy yet feminine and perfect. My hold around her tightens, and she sighs in her sleep, her face nuzzling into my chest. My heart swells—she rolled over in her sleep to get closer to me.

I lay there for a while, unsure if a minute or an hour goes by. All I know is this is what I want for the rest of my life. Her in my arms, her hair fanned across my pillow, her soft breath against my skin. I never want to go a day without touching her, kissing her, smelling her perfume. I've never loved someone so much that I'd let them drown me, consume me, *destroy* me, but for her... for her, I'd do anything. Before her, I only remember emptiness—the kind that hatred carves deep inside your soul, that eats you alive slowly until all you can think of is death and revenge. But this... this love, this woman, *this witch*, bursted into my life and made me *thirst* as if I'd been starved and dehydrated for eternity. As if she were the last drop of water. As if she were the last morsel of nourishment. As if she were the last breath of air.

And maybe she is. Maybe she's all of those things because I've never needed anything as much as I need her beside me.

Bending my head down, I kiss the top of her head. Her hair is smooth as silk against my lips and smells like cloves. I lightly brush the hair off her face, tracing the line of her cheek and jaw with one finger, reveling in her softness.

Slowly, I force myself to slip out of bed and make my way downstairs. Opening the kitchen window, I talk to Kaylus about what happened last night, though he'll have to talk to Adara for a two-sided conversation. He flies upstairs while I start coffee and breakfast, wanting her to have everything at her fingertips the moment she wakes up.

A soft thud hits the floor, and I turn to face the doorway. Adara stands there, fidgeting with her sweatshirt sleeves, a duffel bag at her feet. I quirk a brow at her, leaning back against the counter.

"I'm going to... go." She avoids eye contact, glancing over her shoulder at the front door. "I called for a ride."

"Well, I guess you better cancel it." I grab my mug off the counter, taking a sip of the hot black drink.

Her gaze flicks to mine, her lips parted. "I can't stay here, Gideon."

"Why?" I set my mug down roughly, the ceramic smacking on the countertop. "Because I think it's the best option to keep you *alive*. You need to stay here so I can protect you, Adara."

"Because it's not safe! If it keeps me alive, then it's only at the cost of *your* life!"

I stalk toward her, dipping my head low to hold her gaze, keeping only an inch of space between us. "Do you think I'm so weak I can't defend myself?" I ask, my voice low. "Do you think I'm delusional in thinking no danger would come here and that's what makes it safe here for you?"

She takes a step back, trying to create space between us, but I follow her, backing her up against the wall.

"Do you think I'd let anything—anyone—come in here and hurt you or myself? Because, darling, anyone who comes here signs their own death certificate the minute they challenge me or come for you."

"You're an arrogant idiot," she says softly.

My brows furrow as her anger rises, her jaw tensing as she glares at me.

"You can't beat her. She's hellbent on killing me, killing all of us. She wants to be immortal. She threatened Jules just to get to me. She threatened you!" She shoves one finger into my chest, tears pricking at her eyes. "She's coming for me, and that means she's coming for *you*. She'll kill you, just like she did last night." Both her palms slap against my chest, and she shoves me back, reaching for her duffel bag.

I grab her wrist, putting her hand on my chest as I pull her back to me. She rips from my grasp, rearing back to slap me, but I catch her arm. "Adara," I whisper, my other hand reaching up, my knuckles brushing her cheek. "Is that why the bed burned last night? Were you fighting her... for me?"

Sharply turning her head away, her chest heaves up and down, her breaths becoming rapid.

"I don't want you to leave," I say, and she looks up at me, tears tracking down her cheeks. "I want you to stay here. With me. Where we can fight *together*."

I pull her into a hug, kissing the top of her head, then guide her to a stool in the kitchen and set food and coffee before her. We eat in silence, and I can't stop thinking about last night and the way she keeps saying I'm not safe if she stays here, as if I'm her biggest concern.

*Yeah, her biggest weakness,* my wolf scoffs. *How do you expect to fight together if you're always worried about keeping the other safe?*

I try to ignore him, but the truth remains the same—if we were attacked, I'd lay my life down to save her. But can either of us survive if we sacrifice ourselves to save the other?

My phone buzzes on the counter, and I snatch it off, seeing a text from Frank about the bar. Quickly, I type a text back.

*Put a rotation on Adara's house. I want to know everything that happens there. If the ashes of the home blow in the wind, I want to know what time and in what direction. Understand?*

*Got it, boss. I'll send the first team now.*

Setting my phone down on the counter with a sigh, Adara heads upstairs without a word, and I hear the shower turn on a moment later. I hang my head, running a hand through my hair. That evil bitch, Monique, is up to something, and I'm going to find out what it is.

## CHAPTER ELEVEN
*Adara*

AFTER TURNING ON THE WATER, I LEAVE THE door open and walk back into the bedroom to sit down on the bed, but a pile of ash stares back at me. I blink back the tears threatening to escape, annoyed at myself for how much crying I've done lately. Sighing, I lean back against the dresser, waiting for the steam from the water to prove the shower is ready.

The early afternoon sun shines through the window, reflecting off Kaylus's feathers as he swoops inside. He glides to the nightstand table, settling himself into his nest that's still standing despite the proximity to last night's fire.

A soft buzzing comes from behind me, and I turn to grab the silver communicator, a new message blinking across its small screen.

*I can be there in twenty,* Chloe texts.

Groaning, I pick up the device and send her a text. *Don't bother. It's fine.*

*Are you sure? I have news.*

Dread curls in my gut. *What news?*

The communicator is silent until Chloe's text comes through, and my stomach drops. *Monique is gone. She shut the whole office down for a month-long vacation.*

Monique never takes vacations. She doesn't believe in respite, relaxing, or doing anything other than being productive and making money. Unless she's taking time off to dive more into the hunt… for me.

Chloe sends another text. *Jules is doing great, though. Her magic is growing, but she already has an amazing handle on it.*

I smile at the message, glad that something is going right at least. *Are they still hunting?*

Steam starts to flow out of the bathroom's open door, and by the time Chloe's next message comes in, the bathroom mirror is completely fogged. *Yes. Be careful.*

With the office closed, Chloe won't have access to Monique or other coven news unless they notify her directly, which is rare since she isn't close to being a priestess, lower ranked as only a maiden.

Within our coven, under the high priestesses would be priestesses, the huntresses, then maidens. Chloe and I are only maidens, not having the amount of power required to reach a huntress level. My stomach twists, knowing it's a team of huntresses coming after me, the ones responsible for hunting down the lycans.

"*Are you going to shower or stand there and stink all day?*" Kaylus asks, tilting his head at me.

I roll my eyes, tossing the communicator onto the dresser and closing the bathroom door behind me.

Hot water trickles down my back as I step under the spray, and I tip my head back, soaking my hair and letting the water wash away last night's soot. The nightmare clings to my mind like a film, making me feel anxious and itchy, suffocated. I scrub until my skin is raw, as if that'll somehow cleanse me of the image of Monique standing over Gideon's dying body as she hunts for me.

Guilt rips through me as my mind wanders to after that nightmare—after the fire consumed the bed. Gideon's arm wrapped around me brought me the best sleep I've ever had. The warmth of his body pressed to my back and the weight of his arm over me pulled me under a deep sleep, and I woke up feeling rested and renewed. Disappointment had crashed over me when I opened my eyes to find myself alone in his bed, but guilt followed soon after, wishing I didn't have to choose between who I am as a witch and a sister and what I want as Gideon's mate.

My wolf has been quiet since the fire last night, and I'm grateful. I don't know if I can handle hearing her talk about how we should just accept our mate bond and our powers when she obviously doesn't have control over my witch magic.

Because the only way to make this right is to get rid of one—my wolf or my magic.

The rest of the dream comes back to me in a rush, and I remember now that I walked the path, that I got farther than I ever had in the midst of Lockwood Forest. I got close to the well and the witch who guards it—somehow in my sleep.

Does that mean I could find the same path if I searched the woods again?

I rush through my shower, drying off to tell Kaylus.

*"Again with this? We won't find it, Addy. Who knows if it even exists,"* he caws at me from his perch.

"Kaylus, I need to find it. I know the well is there. Why else is that witch guarding it?" I stroke his feathers. "Plus, my grandmother spoke about it. She'd been there herself."

He sighs. *"I don't know... The wolves aren't bad, though—they're nothing like the coven says."* He tilts his head at me. *"You know that more than anyone. They've accepted you."*

Guilt claws at me, knowing I have to either give up this new pack family that I've found or my family with witches, with Jules. "I can't stay here," I whisper. "Monique will find me. She'll find Gideon and use our bond against us somehow. I... I can't put them in that kind of danger."

Kaylus stares at me until I shift my weight uncomfortably.

"My family is Jules. You and her are all I have left," I whisper. "I have to try."

He's silent for a moment, then nods his head slightly. *"Okay, what do you want to do?"*

A relieved smile spreads across my face. "I want to find the witch. I saw her last night, and I think I know what to do this time. I think."

*"What about Gideon? He isn't going to like this."*

I shrug, grimacing. "I know, but I don't have any other choice. This is the only way to keep him safe."

*"You don't think she'll come for him even after you give up your wolf and mate bond?"*

"No," I sigh. "She wants me more than anything. She's left him alone for this long, right?" I ruffle his feathers lightly before moving to the door.

*"Addy?"*

I look over my shoulder at the raven.

*"One day, you're going to need to realize it isn't all black and white. There's a lot of gray in the world. And there's a lot of people who love you. A lot of people worth fighting for."*

I give him a small smile as an ache builds in my chest. Making my way downstairs with a plan to feign being exhausted after last night and skip my shift at the bar, Gideon's voice drifts across the living room to me.

"No, I want the house monitored twenty-four, seven. Overlap the shifts if you have to... I don't care if it's just ashes. It's top priority when the witches are making a move on us, especially this one."

His head snaps over to me as I take the last few steps, my bones heavy and my hands shaking. He's watching my house—Monique's house. I lean against the wall, watching him.

"I'll talk to you later, Frank." He hits a button to end the call, tossing the phone on the couch beside him.

"You're spying on my house?" I raise a brow, trying to muster enough anger to look irritated. "You didn't think to tell me?"

He chuckles, draping an arm across the back of the couch. "Are you the alpha?"

"No, if I was the alpha, I wouldn't be sending my pack on a useless task." I smirk as his gaze narrows at me. "It's pointless watching that place. She never liked being there when her favorite kid was inside, let alone now that it's just a pile of ashes. The perfect reminder of me—her most despised failure."

He sets his jaw, inhaling slowly through his nose. "Don't talk like that."

"Like what? It's the truth. Even if she threatened Jules to get me to surrender, she was still her favorite." Spinning on my heel, I walk into the kitchen and grab a bottle of water, needing something in my hands to fidget with.

His hand clamps down on my shoulder just as I'm twisting off the cap, and he spins me around, taking the bottle from me and slamming it on the counter, water sloshing over the top. "I don't care if you think it's the truth. You don't get to talk about yourself that way." He presses me back against the counter, his hand gripping my hip and the other cupping my neck. His thumb tips my chin up, his black hair falling almost into his eyes. "You are incredible, and I'll use every last breath I have to keep reminding you until you believe it."

I swallow hard, wishing his words didn't hurt like a knife in my heart, twisting deeper with every sweet thing he says to me, because this can't be what I want. This can't be my life. I belong with Jules and Kaylus, gaining control over my powers. Hell, I don't even *want* my powers. I'd rather be low-power, useless Adara Morrow, just as I was before everything was ruined and complicated. Before a target was placed on my back.

He dips his head, his mouth capturing mine in a kiss that sears itself onto my soul, branding into my mind for the rest of my life, and I grab his hips, pulling him closer to me. Because I want to remember everything. How he tastes like whiskey, the way his touch awakens every inch of me, the soft skin at his ribs as my fingers slip under his shirt and drift up.

His hand travels down, both gripping my hips as he lifts me onto the counter, stepping between my legs, and I wrap them around his waist. My hands dive into his hair, running my fingers through the wavy thickness, as I cling onto him with one thought running through my mind.

This man is going to ruin me.

"Mila should be here soon," Gideon says, looking me over as I sit on the couch buried under the fluffiest throw blanket he owns, the place I landed after our heady make out in the kitchen. "I just have to do some interviews for new waitstaff, so I shouldn't be too long."

I push away my nerves of him leaving early to come back here and swallow down my remark that I don't need a gods damn babysitter. "It's fine. Go, work, do your interviews. I'm just... tired after last night." I give him a small smile.

He glances at the clock, then tosses me a cell phone. "Here. Numbers are already programmed. Answer if I text or call you." He licks his lips when I press my lips in a firm line. "Please." He walks over and kisses my temple, making my mouth go dry.

"Okay," I say, nodding. I wait on the couch as I listen to his truck drive down the gravel toward the road. Picking up the cell phone, I send a quick text to Mila that she doesn't need to come since I'm just going to bed.

She sends back a thumbs up, and I set the phone down, smiling to myself. I didn't expect him to give me a phone, but it's worked out even better than I thought now. I don't know if I would've been able to sneak out without Mila noticing if she'd been here.

I grab a small bag packed with a few essentials—water and a change of clothes—putting my phone in the pocket in case Gideon texts me, knowing he'd leave the bar immediately if he did and I didn't answer. I turn off the lights, leaving a small lamp on upstairs as if I were actually going to bed, then make my way into the back yard to find Kaylus.

"That was... easy." He swirls in the air above me as we move through the woods.

I'm grateful I know these woods so well after studying the territory lines of the Silver Wolf Pack. Gideon's house is a smaller trek to Lockwood Forest than my house had been, but not by much. It'll still take roughly an hour to walk there. "Hopefully, it'll stay easy tonight." Glancing up at the star filled sky, I grimace. "At least getting there. Once we get there, keep your distance."

"*I don't like this.*"

I roll my eyes. "Yeah, you said that a few times now, but you know why I have to do this."

"*Yeah, I know why you think you have to.*" He caws, flying a little ahead of me as I strip my clothes off and shift.

I shake out my fur and take off after him, feeling the urge of my wolf to turn around and crawl back into Gideon's bed. Gritting my teeth, I shove her down and push myself faster, feeling the wind ripple through my fur. She still hasn't talked to me again, but I know she's the reason my walls are crumbling when I'm around him. The bond grows between us with every minute spent together, and it makes me crave his touch, his voice, his everything. But with that, my powers are also growing. Training has helped me gain more control of my wolf, but my fire... It still feels unstable, like a true flame—wicked and vengeful with a mind of its own.

I know what I have to do to fix this and keep everyone safe—lose the exact things that make me a target. It's the only way to give myself a normal life with Jules. Even if I'm not a witch, I can still live near her and work in the city. I'm just hoping I won't lose myself when I lose my wolf *and* my fire.

## CHAPTER TWELVE
*Gideon*

*A PHONE DOESN'T SEEM LIKE THE BEST MOVE. YOU know she's going to tell Mila not to show up,* my wolf says.

"That's exactly why I gave it to her. At least I can get ahold of her if she does that. She would've just talked Mila into leaving anyway." Sighing, I turn my truck engine off after parking in the bar's lot. I would've told Frank to handle the interviews himself, but with the new task of watching Adara's house, I didn't want to pile everything on him. Plus, I enjoy handpicking my staff. I need someone I can trust to be at the bar and help Frank, not some self-absorbed redhead like last time.

Cursing myself for my past moment of weakness, I throw open my truck door and stalk inside. A scowl immediately shadows my face as I look through the bar, noting Lucas's band playing on the stage again. At least that's still working out, and the band doesn't hit on my waitresses.

I see Frank at the bar, packed with people, and he laughs as he fills another round of beers for a table.

Walking to the back of the bar, I sidle up to Kurtis at the gambling tables.

"Hey, boss." He shuffles the deck before dealing cards to the four people sitting before him.

"No Wendell tonight?"

Kurtis smirks. "Not since that first night. I heard Anera wasn't very happy about the show he put on."

A dark chuckle bursts from me. "Good to know she continues to keep his leash nice and short." I pat his shoulder as I walk to my office. "Frank, interviews held in here. One at a time."

He glances up at me, pouring a cluster of shots. "Got it, boss. First one's right there," he throws his thumb toward the end of the bar. One of Mila's friends sits there, chewing on her lower lip. He nods his head in my direction, and she jumps up.

"Cali, right?" I ask, leading her into my office.

"Uh, yeah, that's right." She smiles nervously, her dark brown hair pulled back into a ponytail.

"And you want to waitress here?" I step behind my desk, gesturing for her to sit in the chair before me.

She licks her lips, sitting down. "I spend enough time here. Might as well be useful."

I smirk. "That's... honest. There's no drinking on the job, though."

Her face blanches. "Oh... no, that's... that's not what I meant. I-I mean, I do drink when I come here. I just—"

"I get it. What makes you a good fit here?" I lean back in my chair, observing the way her hands toy with the edge of her shirt. "If you're this nervous just talking with me, are you going to be able to work around me?"

Her hands still, and her eyes find mine. She tucks a loose strand of hair behind her ear. "I can multitask, and I honestly just really need this job. I was dating Aaron before..."

My jaw clamps together, my teeth making an audible clack, and she flinches.

"He's been really weird," she says softly. "He stopped... well, everything. Hugging me, kissing me, he barely even talked to me anymore. Until he kicked me out. I moved in with my friend for now, staying on her couch, but I can't even afford to pay her any grocery money right now." She chews on her lower lip for a moment, taking a deep breath. "Gods, I sound pathetic. I was working with him in his friend's auto shop in town. I'd answer the phones and stuff, but once he kicked me out, they replaced me there too. It's..." She wipes away a stray tear, scoffing. "It's humiliating to be erased as if I didn't exist or matter, you know? Almost as humiliating to be dumping all of this on you when you didn't even ask." She looks up, grimacing.

"Can you start tonight?"

Her mouth hangs open. "Are you serious?" Her eyes fill with tears when I nod, and she closes them, blowing out a breath. "Oh my gods." She smiles at me when she opens her eyes. "I'll go out there right now. Thank you, uh, boss."

I nod at the door. "Ask Frank for an apron. He'll show you the ropes."

She smooths a hand over her hair, pulling back her shoulders as she goes back into the crowded bar. Once the door closes behind her, I reach into my desk and grab the bottle of whiskey, drinking from it as I make a mental note to pay Aaron Kilch and his friends a visit.

I get through three more interviews, choosing to hire Lucas's girlfriend, Vera, along with Cali. I almost hire a third, offering Lucas some extra pay instead, if he fills in when he doesn't have a set to play, knowing Adara plans to wait tables whether I allow her to or not.

The thought reminds me to balance my books, so I pull out my notebooks and start that after checking the new security camera I added to my office window. But it shows nothing. Irritated, I focus on the numbers swimming before me on the page. Why leave a note once and not return?

*They're playing with you*, my wolf says.

Growling, I tip back my glass, downing the whiskey and refilling the cup. I know that, but *why* are they playing with me? What game is this?

Pausing my movements, I glare at the window. "Why did you say *they*?" I mumble. "The note only had one initial.

*You have more than one enemy, Gideon.*

I walk over to the window, staring out into the dark night outside. My reflection stares back at me in the glass. "Don't be cryptic. It doesn't suit you when you're normally a blunt ass."

*There's a lot of names that start with A. Aaron. Aramin. Allen. But none of them could make the night air stale and press pause on a breeze.*

My lip curls up when I realize how stupid I was. Of course it wasn't Aramin—she's never been the type to leave a note. She's the type to show up unannounced at the lake and beg for me to take her back. Rathmann's murderous stare from the council meeting sends off alarms in my head. I don't understand why he'd sign that note with his first initial, unless to throw me off his scent on purpose. He knows—he must be watching me.

*And he must be working with a witch.*

Pissed, I know my wolf is right. Only a spell could stop the wind from blowing, stop the breeze from taking that light weight package from where it was strategically placed outside my window. But why would Rathmann be working with a witch if he hates them as much as he does?

Downing the second refill of whiskey, I hurl the rocks glass at the wall. The glass shatters and rains down on the floor as I slump down onto my chair. I rub a finger over my chin, trying to figure out why a witch and a wolf would be working together. Is it just to target me as the alpha? Or is there more to this—to go as far as to include Adara?

I rip my phone off my desk and text her, wanting to make sure she's okay. *Sleeping yet?*

*Not a wink*, she sends back.

I smile at the screen, glad that she didn't fight me on responding quickly like I'd asked. I send her one of those kissy faces before checking the list of hunters Frank gave me. I dial the name written down for tonight—Brent Poltan.

"Hey, boss," he answers on the first ring.

"Update." I pick up a pen, hovering over my notebook, clicking the top of the pen over and over.

"Uh, nothing much really. Ashes look undisturbed at the house. No tracks anywhere. No fresh scents." He angles the phone away from him to speak to someone else, then pulls it back. "Everyone here has the same report, same as day shift too."

"Keep me updated. The minute you see something, you call me."

"You got it."

I hang up, slamming the phone on the desk, and stare at the blank page before sweeping everything off it and into the wall. Gods damn it all, I just want one—*one*—piece of something to go on and know what is happening. What Monique is up to, the coven, the council, Aramin, Kilch. *Everyone.*

Staring at the mess on the floor, I close my eyes and take a deep breath. Gods, this is infuriating.

I'm tempted to go for a run or a swim, and I take two steps toward the door before I stop. *"This isn't pack territory, Dee."* Aramin's words come back to me, words I know are wrong, but something about them nag at me. Pivoting, I head for the bookcase nearest the door, stooping to the bottom shelf to grab a book with gold lettering on its spine.

*Pack Maps of the Country.*

I walk over to my desk, flipping the book open and skimming to the page that relates to New England, then to my pack. The book is organized by area of the country, then by pack, since some packs are small and can be in the same area together. I unfold the spread, finding the X I placed over the bar and the other I placed on my house. Trailing my finger along the map, I find the blue body of water... outside my territory limit.

"What the hell," I mutter.

I check it three more times, questioning the print right before my eyes. I tear into my desk, reaching into the bottom drawer and pulling out the documents from the council the day I took over the last bit of territory, half a century ago. The folder has every territory expansion I've accomplished contained within it, so I pull out my first map along with the most recent.

The first map, its paper thin with ink preserved by magic, shows just the town with a part of the forest, including the lake. Frowning down at the misprint, I compare the latest map from the council—with no lake included, making my territory lines farther east than they were before, ending just before the lake begins.

Technically, I should contact Rathmann about this to clarify territory lines since he's the first point of contact for my pack, but the thought shrivels the minute it forms. Grant will just need to make time to handle this issue himself.

Spreading out the rest of the maps on the desk, I document every small difference that wasn't agreed on over the course of my alpha reign. By the time the bar closes, I have a notebook full of problems for the head councilman to resolve and a raging headache. Anger blurs my vision when I realize how much has changed since I became alpha because of their underhanded tricks, slowly piling up overtime until it gave them exactly what they wanted—a free man territory just west of my pack, where ferals and outlaws could roam without cause or rule.

A fucking nightmare is more accurate, and now that's exactly what Grant is going to deal with—his nightmare. *Me.*

## CHAPTER THIRTEEN
*Adara*

THE BED SHIFTS BENEATH ME AS GIDEON crawls under the covers. I groggily smile as he scoots closer, wrapping his arm around me and pulling me close against him. He nuzzles into my hair and sighs, falling asleep within seconds. It's late, much later than I expected him to come back, but I can't remember anything from before I went to bed.

Yawning, my brows furrow as I try to remember what happened tonight. Thinking back to yesterday, I remember everything that happened... up until I got the phone from Gideon. My mouth goes dry as I remember leaving with Kaylus to find the Lockwood witch, but find myself unable to remember anything after that.

"*Kaylus?*" I reach out to him, his black feathers reflecting the moonlight as he sits on his perch on the windowsill.

"*You're awake,*" he says, his head snapping over to me.

*"Shh, don't move. I don't want to wake him."* The hair on my neck tickles as Gideon's warm breath sighs against me. *"What happened? I... can't remember."*

Kaylus ruffles his feathers, concern lacing through him. *"We found the path..."*

*"What?"* It takes every ounce of control to not bolt upright. *"How did I get back here? Why don't I remember?"*

*"Because we didn't find the well, Addy."* He sighs. *"The witch yelled at us to leave, laughed at you showing up in person to a place you'd only accessed once in a dream. Her voice echoed all around us. You couldn't smell her or hear her enough to track her. Your wolf... wouldn't come out or talk to you until... well, until the witch said you'd lose everything if you stayed."*

My throat tightens, frustration rising inside me and mixing with my fear that I'll never fix this. That I'll bring suffering to everyone I love no matter what I do. Rolling over, I bury my face in Gideon's chest. Swallowing back my tears, I force myself to go back to sleep, hoping that I'll end up in the same place I'd searched for tonight. Lockwood Forest.

*Smoke swirls around me, carrying the scent of burned paper. Orange glowing embers float in the air, the only glimpse of light in the darkened space. Coughing, I lift a hand to my face, trying to wave the smoke away, but it's useless. The haze is too thick.*

*"I told you not to come back here!" an angry, shrill voice yells. Her words echo around me, and I spin in a circle trying to find her.*

*"I just want to find the well—"*

*Her cackling laugh cuts me off, and my mouth goes dry. "You want to give up the gifts the gods have given you, child. Don't be foolish."*

*"Gifts?" I say, incredulous. "You don't know anything about me or my gifts! This life has been nothing but a curse."*

*"You can't see the forest for the trees." The witch appears before me, her face too hazy to see any details, but her frame is small. Her hair appears to be moving like living flames, bright orange and flowing in the air around her.*

*"I need to get rid of this—all of it." I try to take a step toward her, but my feet won't move. Glancing down at them, I see thick vines growing around my ankles, keeping me glued in place. "Please! You don't understand. They're all going to die—"*

*"No," she snaps. "You don't understand the cost of the wish you're looking to make." Her blurry image darts forward until her face is mere inches from my own. Her deep blue eyes look like an inky night sky, the reflecting embers in her irises blinking and floating like meteors falling—shooting stars. "They only die if you let them," she hisses.*

*I open my mouth to argue, because she has no idea what she's talking about, no idea what my powers are or the danger they pose to those around me, but it's pointless. She casts me from the forest—again. The hazy woods swirl around me, and I scream in frustration.*

---

Gideon shakes my shoulder. "Adara!"

Blinking the bright sunlight from my eyes, I turn my face toward him. My throat is sore when I swallow, and my eyes burn from the smoke-filled clearing.

"You were screaming," he says, brushing a finger down my cheek. He gently kisses my forehead and pulls back to look at me with worried eyes. "What happened?"

"N-nothing," I stutter, my voice hoarse.

His eyes narrow at me, disbelief evident in his features.

"I can't remember the dream. I only remember... being angry." I try to offer some vague detail, hoping it's enough to convince him into letting it go.

"Mm, if you didn't want to talk about it, you could just say that." He gives a small smirk, one side of his mouth lifting slightly, then kisses my cheeks and gets out of bed. "I have an appointment, but I'll see you later. Mila will come by for training."

My brows furrow. "Mila? But I thought you were..." I want to swallow the words as they leave my mouth. Why am I so disappointed at not spending the day with him? I should be grateful, not having him here will allow me more control over my powers, but instead all I can focus on is that he's going alone. "Is Frank not going with you?"

He laughs, pulling on a button-up shirt and turning toward me. "Do I need a bodyguard for an appointment?"

I scowl at him, crossing my arms over my chest to keep from reaching for him. "Depends what kind of appointment you have."

"Nothing that I can't handle myself." He rounds the bed, cupping my cheek as he brushes his lips over mine before kissing me. "I'll meet you at the bar after so you can meet the new staff. Now get dressed. I hear Mila pulling in."

His gaze travels over me, his t-shirt grazing the tops of my thighs, and my cheeks heat at the fire in his eyes. I wait until he walks downstairs before rummaging through my clothes to get dressed for training. Excitement flutters through me at the thought of training with Mila. Last time, her speed was faster than I could track her scent, and I want to see if I can track her better today. If I can, maybe I can track my way to the Lockwood well too... or at least to the witch who guards it. After getting dressed, I go downstairs and pour a cup of coffee, Mila closing the door behind her as I lift the mug to my lips.

"Hey, girl," she says, smiling. "You ready for this?"

I smile back at her, her cheer hard to resist, then follow her outside. Standing in the grass after setting my coffee down on a side table, I look up at her.

"Okay, let's practice what we did the first time. Draw out your claws—only your claws."

I keep my eyes open, drawing inside myself and pulling my wolf forward. She's become more complacent since I set my bed on fire the other day, choosing not to talk to me but also not fight against my shifts. I fight the frown pulling at my lips as my nails lengthen into claws effortlessly.

"Wow, that's a great improvement," Mila cheers.

I retract them, shaking my hands out. "Can we work on tracking today?"

Her eyebrows raise, her shock apparent. "Uh, sure, but I'm not on the hunter team, so it'll be pretty basic."

I nod, smiling. "That's fine with me."

After a couple of hours of the most intense game of hide-and-seek, I collapse onto the lounge chair. Mila lays on the one next to me, laughing.

"How can you hide your scent so well?" I ask between breaths.

She looks at me with a glint in her eyes. "I use the wind."

"The wind?" I ask, chugging the bottle of water she tosses to me.

She nods. "Yep. I stand downwind, making sure that whoever I'm hiding from is upwind of me so the breeze won't carry my scent."

"Wow," I say, laughing breathlessly. "That... is really smart."

"What? Did you think I was all looks, no brain?" She squirts me with her water bottle.

"No," I say quickly, squealing at the cold water soaking into my shirt. "Okay, maybe a little." I laugh when she sprays me again, then run inside to grab a towel to dry off.

I grab my phone off the side table in the living room and check for messages from Gideon. The blank notifications bar stares back at me, and worry weeds in my mind. My fingers hover over the keys, wondering if I should text him. It's almost noon, and he said he wanted to meet at the bar after whatever he was doing. Looking through the slider door at Mila sunbathing on the lounge chair, I wonder if she knows anything about his plans. Did Frank tell her anything? I let out a breath. Probably not, honestly. Frank wouldn't tell anyone Gideon's business unless he felt it was unavoidable and necessary.

I toss the phone back on the couch and poke my head out the back door. "I'm going to take a shower.

Feel free to use the downstairs bathroom if you want one."

She cracks open one eye, smirking at me. "Yeah? Thanks for the invitation. You're a great hostess, almost like you live here or something."

Heat colors my cheeks, and I roll my eyes as I walk away, heading upstairs.

---

I fidget with the seatbelt as we drive to the bar. Mila offered to drop me off—insisted on it, really, since she knew I didn't have any other ride. The trees race past the window, a low hanging fog clinging to the dark, wet bark. Fall always brings this eerie weather, and I'm grateful for the clothes Mila's loaned me as I pull my hands inside the sweatshirt's sleeves to stave off the chill.

"I know Cali isn't supposed to work until a bit later today, so I'm not sure why he wanted you to come in so early." Mila fiddles with the radio stations, switching from alternative rock to country hits. Garth Brooks pours from the stereo for a minute before she changes it again to a today's hits station, bobbing her head along to Taylor Swift's latest pop song.

"Cali is working here now?" I ask, wondering why Gideon didn't mention her last night. But I push off the burst of jealousy because I can't keep my claim on him. I have to get rid of this wolf and our mate bond.

Mila nods. "Yep. She started last night, I guess. She's had it rough ever since Aaron dumped her, so I'm glad Gideon gave her a break."

"Aaron?" The image of the drummer from a few weeks ago pops into my head, Gideon dragging him outside. A chill snakes down my spine.

"Yeah, one and the same, girl." She throws me a sad, knowing smile. "She's better off without him, honestly, but the way he's just ghosted her is bullshit after how long they'd been dating."

"I... I didn't realize he even had a girlfriend with the way he... you know." I avoid her gaze, keeping my eyes glued to the trees outside, my vision becoming unfocused as I think about him, the way he touched me, the way he spoke about Aramin.

"Yep. Class A douchebag." A new song comes on the radio, and she turns up the dial. "Oh, I love this one!" She dances along to the song, and I laugh, joining in with her as we drive the last bit of distance to the bar.

I feel happy as I exit the car, but a crushing sadness overtakes me as I watch her drive away. Once I get rid of my wolf, I won't be able to see her anymore. As a witch, or even a human, I won't be allowed in lycan territory again, especially the Silver Wolf territory. The bar door creaks open behind me, and I brush off the depression clinging to my mind.

Gideon stands in the doorway, leaning against the frame. "You coming inside, little witch? Or are you gonna stand here staring at the fog all night?"

I roll my eyes at him, trying to squash the burst of joy that courses through me at seeing him. "I'm coming. I'm coming."

He holds open the door, and I try to squeeze by him to get inside, but his hand rests on my side, pulling me close as I pass him. "You look incredible," he whispers into my hair.

I lick my lips, brushing my hair back from my face. "Oh, thanks." I smile sheepishly up at him, realizing he hasn't seen me in jeans before. The jeans Mila loaned me are tight, hugging every curve of my body, and the low v-neck shirt I paired with it only enhances all my other curves. I clear my throat, looking around the empty bar. "Wasn't I supposed to meet the other people you hired?"

The corner of his mouth quirks. "You will. Later. But I have some things to do around here and thought you might enjoy helping me. Well." He glances around the bar briefly before looking back down at me. "I thought I might enjoy watching you help me."

I follow him toward the bar, slipping behind the counter and watching him grab a bucket.

"I need to clean the tops of those shelves up there," he gestures to the very top, up by the ceiling. "I can't reach on my own, and although I could get a ladder, holding you above me so you can reach would be much more fun." A mischievous gleam sparks in his eyes.

After wetting a cloth, he lifts me up by my waist, his hands hot as branding rods on my body. I struggle to focus on my task of dusting and wiping off each shelf, the task taking more focus than it should've. I never would've been able to clean Monique's house with this man around. After the last shelf, he sets me down. I look up at them to study my work, and my face scrunches up.

"I missed a spot," I say, reaching to rinse the cloth off so I can reuse it.

"It's fine," Gideon says, moving to grab a drink for each of us.

I turn to look at him. "But I missed it?"

He looks at the spot I point to, then back at me. "It's barely noticeable, Adara. It's fine."

"But—"

"I said it's fine. Now will you please take a break and drink something?" He holds the glass of soda toward me.

I toss the cloth into the suds bucket and take the offered drink, feeling inadequate at my one, incredibly simple task.

Gideon sets his glass down, sliding over to me. "I asked you to clean them, and you did. I didn't, and wouldn't, ask you to spit shine them until they gleam under these pathetic lights."

My tongue darts out to lick my lips, tears threatening to spill from my eyes.

"It's fine, okay? You did a great job. Exactly what we needed to do."

He stares into my eyes until I whisper, "Okay," then kisses me softly.

"I have to clean up the break room in the back. Stay here..." he takes my hand and pulls me around the bar, "sit," then sets my soda on the bar top, "and relax with your drink." He steps back, then narrows his gaze at me. "No arguments."

Before I can open my mouth, he uses his speed to get to the back of the bar. I don't miss the smirk he throws over his shoulder at me before he disappears down the hall. It's not long before a knock comes from the bar door. It's locked since it's after hours, but a small part of me wonders if it's Cali. Maybe Mila told her I was already here so she came to help clean.

Scooting off the stool, wondering who else Gideon hired, I take a few steps to the door and swing it open. My breath catches in my throat when patchouli hits my nose, and my eyes adjust to the bright sun—perfectly tamed blonde curls, expertly painted red lips, and piercing green eyes stare at me from the other side of the door. Her nose is turned up in disgust as she looks down at me.

"I knew you'd be here," Monique sneers, pushing past me into the bar. She looks around the low lit space, dragging a finger over the bar top and rubbing the nonexistent dirt between two fingers.

## CHAPTER FOURTEEN
*Gideon*

DEEP CLEANING THE BAR IS THE ONE THING I never delegate. I love being here when it's empty, when I can play any song I want on the bluetooth speakers, when I can get lost in thinking that I'm not the alpha of my pack. It makes me feel normal, like my biggest concern is whether I cleaned out all the old containers in the fridge and scrubbed the sink thoroughly enough.

Today, however, my visit with Grant takes over my thoughts. Raymond Grant is the biggest bastard, which is never surprising. It takes a special breed of bastard to lead the other assholes without being constantly challenged for your position at the head.

I caught him by surprise this morning, waiting to catch him on the road heading toward the council lodge. I sat in the middle of the pavement, flicking my tail and patiently waiting for his driver to stop the car. Grant recognized me immediately, throwing open the back passenger door with a sigh.

"What is it now, Disantollo?" he'd asked impatiently.

I stood just outside the door, snarling at his laid back posture on the backseat of the black sedan. *"I want to know what's happening with my territory lines."*

He raised a brow at me, a smug grin splitting his face. "Ah, so you've finally caught onto that."

*"What the hell is going on?"* I growled, my jowls dripping onto his leather seat.

His gaze flicked down at the saliva in distaste. "I wanted an unclaimed territory separating our council from your... mongrel pack." He waved his hand in the air, as if swatting away a fly.

*"You think my pack is full of mongrels? What do you think is breeding in that free range territory you've created, Grant?"* I placed one paw on the leather seat, letting my claws pierce the thick fabric, tearing large gashes into it. *"If we're mongrels, then what do you call a councilman working with a witch?"*

His head swiveled toward me, anger written on his face. "Don't make accusations you yourself are guilty of."

A dark laugh escapes me. *"Go ask Rathmann about the love note he left for me. Let me know how well you trust him after that."*

Pushing off the leather seat, tearing the fabric down to the base, I darted back into the woods.

Now, in the breakroom, I scowl as I look into the fridge. This council is becoming more corrupt with every decade that passes, corrupt and unpredictable. A combination that will never sit well with me.

My ears perk up as I hear the metal of the bar door clank shut. No one should be here until later tonight when the bar opens. I step out into the hall, keeping to the shadows as voices drift toward me.

"What... what do you want?" Adara asks, her hand still on the door as she keeps her distance from the tall blonde.

*Witch,* my wolf snarls.

"What? No *how are you, Mother?* No *I'm sorry for burning down your house and ripping away your gifted daughter?*" the other woman asks, arrogance seeping off her in waves.

Adara scoffs. "I don't have anything to apologize for, and I especially don't have anyone to call Mother."

Her mother sighs, shaking her head. "I want you to come home. Is that so terrible?"

"No, I'm never..." Adara says warily, narrowing her eyes at her. "You're hunting me for the coven, so why are you here alone."

My body tenses at her words. The coven is hunting her, and she knew—she knew and didn't tell me. She also knew her mother was a part of the hunt.

Her mother laughs, the sound like nails dragging down glass. "I'm not only hunting you for the coven, Adara, I'm leading the hunt." She turns, taking a glance around the bar, sneering in disgust. "Come home, and we can talk to the other priestesses about a deal for you. Let us experiment on you, and they'll probably let you live."

Adara's hand on the door tightens, her knuckles turning white. "You know those experiments are a death sentence. I'll die either way."

Shrugging, her mother smirks and tosses her curls over one shoulder. "You're right, that's no way to make you come home, is it? I should've started with, we'll let Juliana live. Is that better?"

Silver flashes through Adara's eyes, and I bite back the urge to rush to her... At least until she's in true danger. I want her to see that her mother isn't anything more than a mouthy witch, that she's capable of standing up to her on her own.

"Is that not enough?" Her mother sighs dramatically and purses her lips. "I can't make much promise for your... delightful taste in men, but I could...

wait, I suppose. If your experiment is successful, we won't need to kill him after all."

"You leave them alone, you—"

"Now, don't get all worked up on me. I do have this," her mother holds up a piece of paper. "It would cover Juliana's tuition. Isn't that the only reason you started working here in the first place?"

Hesitation flicks across Adara's eyes, and I refuse to watch this witch play games with her any longer. I clear my throat as I walk from the shadows, right into the bar. Both women turn to face me, Adara's face losing all color as she glances between me and her mother, whose lips pucker sourly.

"You know, it's funny," I say, walking over to Adara and grabbing her hand. I pull her tight against me, facing her mother with a grin. "I believe that bill is already paid."

"What—" her mother sputters, her eyes narrowing at me.

"Hard to use a paid bill as leverage, unfortunately. Juliana Morrow's tuition is paid in full—for her *entire* education. Room and board too, of course." Pure pleasure ripples through me at the look on her mother's face. "Now, I believe it's time for you to leave." I hold open the door, waiting for her mother to collect her shattered thoughts and pick her jaw up from the floor.

Her eyes snap from my face to Adara, who shrinks back. Her mother's hand whips out, but I grab her wrist just before the slap makes contact, yanking her close. I stare down at her, a breath between our faces.

"If you ever think of laying a hand on her again," I hiss under my breath, silver overtaking my eyes as I let my claws lengthen and pierce into the tender flesh at her wrist, "I will gladly tear you apart. She's the only reason you're still standing here."

Monique's gaze flicks to Adara for a moment before she blows out a breath, plastering a fake smile on her face and running a hand over her curls. "Well, I never expected it to play out quite like this." Turning her face to me, her smile grows, wicked and malicious. "No more fog clouding your mind, Disantollo?"

She smirks, and I toss her out of the door, slamming it shut behind her. I lock the door, turning back and wrapping my arms around Adara's shaking shoulders.

"Are you okay?" I ask her.

She buries her face in my shirt, nodding slightly. "She has magic, Gideon. A door isn't enough—"

"The bar is protected. No spells with the intent to harm can be cast here. You let her in, didn't you?"

She pulls her head back to look up at me, regret painting her face.

"I'm no fool. I know how magic operates, little witch." I run a hand down her hair, smoothing it back from her face. "I had an old friend protect this bar with a spell long ago. The only witch I've ever trusted. Well..." My thumb brushes over her lips. "My circle seems to have grown by one."

"Were you serious? About Jules?" Her eyes search mine, her voice almost worried to ask.

"Of course I was. It's been paid for, with a lovely note signed in your name that stated it includes a donation to the academy itself. I did pay a bit early, though, so she won't have to wait until fall to attend. She can start this winter, early acceptance with the room and board available whenever she wants it." I smile as a gasp escapes her.

She jumps up onto her toes, wrapping her arms around my neck. "Why would you do that?" she asks, tears wetting the collar of my shirt.

I laugh, burying one hand in her hair and rubbing her back with the other. "Because I didn't want this to happen. Your mother doesn't deserve to have leverage over you, and this was the only way you'd be tempted to leave with her. For others, not for yourself."

She loosens her grip, sliding her hands to each side of my face as she pulls my lips down to hers. I lose myself in her scent, her taste. In the fact that she kissed me and not the other way around. She presses against me, and I spin with her, pressing her back against the door. Her fingers slide into my hair, pulling me closer as she deepens the kiss. She parts her lips, opening for me, her tongue meeting mine stroke for stroke.

I fist her hair, the silky smooth strands slipping perfectly between my fingers, and brush my other hand down her body, gripping her hip. I press into her, wanting no space left between us, no air, no breath. She moans lightly into my mouth, and my wolf breaks free. My claws lengthen, digging into her jeans, and I nip at her bottom lip, licking the small bead of blood that forms. Her wide silver eyes gaze up at me, her chest panting as she tries to catch her breath, her hands still tightly clinging to my hair.

"Tell me what you want, *mia fiamma*," I say, my lips brushing against hers as I speak. "Tell me you want me." I work to catch my own breath, knowing I want her—all of her, all over me. But I won't take her without her telling me I can. I want her to give herself over to me. My tongue licks along her bottom lip, and her eyes dip to my mouth.

"I-I want you," she whispers. Her eyes look up at mine. "I want you, Gideon."

Desire flares through me, and my wolf is near howling in my chest as I crush my mouth to hers, my hands palming her ass as I lift her up. She wraps her legs around my waist, sealing her body to mine, as I carry her through the bar. Reaching the closed office door, I press her against the wood. My lips trail from her mouth, planting kisses along her jaw and down her neck to her shoulder. I nip at the exposed flesh of her collarbone, brushing my tongue over it. Dipping my head low, I drag my tongue along the edge of her shirt, dipping it between her cleavage as she arches into me, her head dropping back against the door.

She whimpers, her grip in my hair tightening, pulling me closer. I reach down, twisting the doorknob and shoving the door open and kicking it closed behind me as I carry her to my desk. My lips never leave hers as I sweep the top of the desk clear and set her on it. She stares up at me, breathless, her lips swollen from kissing, and her eyes widen as I finger the hem of her shirt. Pulling it up reveals the smooth skin of her stomach, and her breath hitches when my thumb brushes her bra, slipping beneath the wire to touch the silky swell of her breast.

Dragging her shirt up and over her head, I let my hand wander to her back, unclasping her bra, and cup her breast, watching her suck her bottom lip into her mouth as a small moan escapes. Lowering my head, I suck one nipple into my mouth, her moan turning into a whimper as my fingers roll and pinch the other one.

Placing my palm to her chest, pushing her back, I trail my finger down, caressing over her stomach as she lays down before me. Her back arches as I lean back down, recapturing her breast in my mouth as I slide my hands down her waist, reaching the button of her jeans. I quickly realize these are the jeans from hell—or a mother expecting celibacy while her daughter tempts the devil. They're so tight I can't pull them in any direction, and it's her next moan as my tongue flicks her nipple that has me letting out my claws, slicing the ridiculous fabric off.

She gasps, her eyes snapping open. "Gideon!" she scolds.

"Darling, the only way you get to say my name right now is if you scream it," I say, letting my hands brush along her thighs.

"I-I..." Her voice wavers the higher I go.

"You what?" I ask, my voice low.

"I just got those," she whispers, closing her eyes as my knuckles brush along the front of her already damp thong.

"Oh? Well, I can always go find you a new pair..." I pull away, smirking as her hand shoots out and grabs my wrist. My fingertips dance over her skin, tracing along the dips of where her thighs meet her hips, and I curl one finger into the seam of her thong and tug it down.

She swallows, her lips parting at the touch, and I crouch down, kissing each inner thigh.

"I have been dying to find out if you taste as good as you smell." I drag my tongue along her thigh, right to her center. Slowly pushing one finger inside her, I dance my tongue around her clit, circling it. "Gods, you are so wet." I suck her clit into my mouth, using my tongue to apply more pressure as my finger thrusts faster inside her.

Adara whimpers, her hips raising to meet me. I wrap my free arm around her, keeping her in place.

She writhes beneath me, squirming closer and closer. "Gideon," she begs, breathless.

I pull my finger out as I stand, dipping it into my mouth and sucking her wetness from it. She bites her lip as she watches me, and the mere taste of her almost sends me over the edge. If her blood was lifesaving, I don't even know if I could put words to how her desire tastes on my tongue. I suck in a breath, staring down at her.

Her body trembles, and I lean over, pausing as I hover above her. She raises shaky hands to my hips, yanking on my shirt until it lifts over my head and is discarded on the floor. She takes her time, tracing the contours of my chest and stomach with her fingers before her eyes swallow me in a galaxy of violet and silver.

A chill snakes down my spine at the gentle whisper of her touch, the heated trail her fingers leave behind as they caress every exposed inch of me. When she fumbles with the button of my pants, I'm close to bringing out my claws again, but I fight back the urge, wanting to experience her touch, drawing out every moment possible. A breath escapes me in a hiss when she reaches into my pants, wrapping her hand around my length. Using one hand, I push my pants to the floor and cup the back of her neck with the other, bringing her up to meet me as I capture her mouth with mine.

I bring my hand between us, dipping my finger into her wet center, and she moans into my mouth. I suck her lip, devouring her moan, her everything. She wriggles, her hips moving as her back arches into me, her breasts pressing into my bare chest. I relish in the feel of her, bringing my hips forward to press my tip against her entrance. I grip her thighs, sliding her down the desk as I press into her. She gasps as I fill her, and I kiss her lips gently until I'm completely buried inside her—a cord snapping so tight in my chest that stars dance in my vision. The mate bond sears itself into my soul, stealing every breath from my lungs.

"Gideon," she gasps against my lips, her hands tangling into my hair.

I slowly pull out, her walls tightening around me, then I thrust back in, finding a rhythm. Wrapping her hair around my fist, I pull gently until she tips her head back to expose her neck. My lips cover her in kisses, biting and licking, and my breaths turn heavy. "Be a good little witch and come for me, *mia fiamma*," I whisper into her ear, gripping her hair as I pump harder, faster, into her, fueled by her sounds and the feel of her hands wandering my body.

Her walls clench around me again, and I claim her mouth, reaching around to grab her ass and tilt her hips up, allowing me deeper access. I thrust into her again and again until she cries out, her nails raking down my back, making me come along with her.

Gods damn fates giving me this witch as my mate... It might be the one thing I actually thank them for.

## CHAPTER FIFTEEN
*Adara*

MY CHEEKS FLAME EVERY TIME I CATCH Gideon's gaze while I wait on the tables, the memory of earlier as fresh in my mind as the soreness between my legs and the pressure in my chest—the mate bond. The bar is packed as usual, and Cali is waiting on the gambling tables as I take over the others. I recognized her as the brunette from Mila's usual friend group the last time I saw them all here, and I'm grateful that it's her and not someone else. Someone like Aramin.

Cali bounces past me to the bar, her chestnut ponytail sways in front of me, and she bumps my shoulder with hers when I step up next to her. "Hey, lady. Your tables good?"

"Yeah," I say. "You need help back there?" I look over at the dark green felt tables, eyeing the greasy haired man holding a cigar. His eyes sweep across the bar as he swivels on his stool, leaning back against the table. Then, he finds me. His hungry gaze lazily travels from my feet up to my face, and he smiles when he catches my stare. I dart my eyes away, feeling the revolting sensation of his eyes still on me.

"Nah, I'm all set." Cali grabs a tray and sets the round of beers on it, then throws a wink over her shoulder at me. "Wendell knows better than to hit on me. I'm a regular at Anera's shop, and I'd tell her in an instant if he slipped up."

I watch her walk back to the other end of the bar, trying to ignore the slimy feeling of Wendell's eyes on me. Grabbing some fresh beers, I drop them off at my tables before heading back to the bar when a hand snakes around my wrist, yanking me into a dark corner. I yelp in surprise, relaxing as Gideon's scent surrounds me. He smells like whiskey and the smoke of the bar, and as his arms wrap around me, I cling to him, grateful to have something familiar, something safe.

I smile into his shirt, hiding my face when I think back to the way his hands traveled over my skin, the way his mouth claimed so many parts of me as his, the way I wanted him to—begged him to.

"Why are you still insisting on working these shifts when you don't have a tuition to pay for anymore?" he says against my ear. His breath tickles the few strands of hair that escaped my bun.

I shiver at the sensation. "I'm not just going to sit around and do nothing."

"Who ever said you'd sit around doing nothing?"

I lift my head to look at him, a smirk painted on his face with hooded eyes. My cheeks flame at the thought, and I move to step back. "I should get back—"

Dipping his head as he pulls me in, he cuts me off with a searing kiss. His lips press firmly to mine, tongue licking the seam of my lips until I open for him to deepen it. His hold on my waist tightens, and my hands cling to his shoulders. His fingers brush the skin under my shirt, grazing over my waist, and I pull back, glancing around the full bar. He chuckles. "No one can see us here," he says. "I made this corner dark on purpose, so I can watch the bar in peace."

My gaze catches on the only person staring at us despite that, and I turn back to Gideon, trying to ignore the sickening twist in my gut at knowing Wendell saw us. I try to give a small smile, but Gideon's brows cinch, then he looks up past my shoulder at the card tables. The light gray of his eyes is immediately swallowed up by silver, giving his eyes an eerie glow in the dimness of the shadows that we're swallowed up in. I reach for his forearm, but he's gone, having used his speed to reach the back of the bar before I could register what was happening.

The bar goes silent as a loud crash comes from the card tables, Gideon throwing the blackjack table Wendell was sitting at moments ago. Cards go flying, raining down on the ground like slowly drifting snowflakes, and a growl tears from Gideon's throat as he stalks toward Wendell, who's now sprawled on the floor, having fallen off his stool.

"B-b-boss," he says, scrambling back.

"Scum," Gideon snarls. "I should've gotten rid of you decades ago." His body trembles, and his nails lengthen to claws, his skin rippling as fur starts to sprout. "Your wife begged me not to, but now what excuse do you have?" He stalks after Wendell, ripping stools and chairs out of his way. "You know she's claimed, though at least this time you know she's over eighteen."

Bile rises in my throat, remembering the blue book. *Wendell, wife caught cheating.* With underage *girls*?

"Y-you know that girl didn't press ch-charges—"

"It's still statutory," Gideon says, his voice deep and threatening. "It's still against pack law."

"I-I fixed this with my wife, boss. She—"

"I don't care!" Gideon roars, flipping a second table. He lunges forward, grabbing the front of Wendell's shirt. "You've let your miry disgraceful eyes roam Adara's body ever since she walked in that door, and it ends here."

Wendell nods feverishly. "I-I'll never look at her again. I—" He whimpers as Gideon drags him toward the bar door, the crowd parting easily, eager to get out of their alpha's way.

"Shift!" Gideon yells, tossing him hard onto the ground.

"W-what?" Wendell sputters, looking around him as if searching for support.

The bar crowd pours toward the door, and I push my way to the front. I find Frank and grip onto his forearm. "Stop him," I say, pleading. "He's going to kill him, isn't he? Stop him!" My voice rises with each word, panic clawing up my throat.

Frank grimaces, patting my hand with his. "No one can stop him once he gets like this."

"No... you..." I struggle to find the words to say, my gaze flicking to Gideon's body as he shifts into his wolf, prowling back and forth as he waits for Wendell.

"Come on," Frank says, pulling from my grasp to wrap his arm around my shoulders. He starts to steer me back inside. "Let's get you inside, okay? Gideon'll be fine."

I let him guide me a few steps before my wolf speaks for the first time in so long that it shocks me, freezing me to the spot.

*Stop him.*

I don't need to know why she's suddenly speaking to me. All I know is that this is *wrong*, and she agrees. I tear from Frank's grasp and whirl around, throwing myself through the crowd. Wendell shifts, his bloated, greasy wolf shaking with his tail between his legs, staring down at the ground. Gideon's muscles coil as he readies to attack, and I stumble, pushing through the last row of the gathered group of people.

Falling onto my hands and knees, I feel the loose gravel cut into my palms.

"Gideon!" I scream, my throat burning. "Stop, don't!" I shove myself up from the ground, latching myself onto his back as he lunges at the other wolf. I dig my hands into his black fur, squeezing my eyes shut as his jaws snap around at me. "Don't do this," I plead, my voice a hoarse whisper as I repeat the words over and over. "Don't do this. Don't make me watch you do this."

Slowly, his body stills beneath me, lowering himself to the ground. His fur disappears, and he twists, wrapping his arms around me as he lays on the ground, shielding me from the crowd. Tears of relief pour out of me, sobs wracking my body as my shoulders shake. I bury my face in his bare chest, my hands clinging to him as if he isn't real.

"Shh," he soothes, smoothing a hand down my hair. "I'm sorry. I'm sorry, *mia fiamma*." His head snaps up, his body tensing as he rolls me onto my back.

*No!* my wolf yells, and my hands move up to his neck before I register the movements.

A scream tears from my lips as Wendell's sharp teeth sink into my flesh, my hands and fingers going numb with fire. Gideon shifts in an instant, ripping the wolf's jaws from my hands as he grows between us. He wrestles Wendell's wolf, jaws snapping. Large arms cradle me under my shoulders and knees, moving me away from the fight as the two black wolves clash against each other in a blur of teeth and claws.

It's a matter of seconds bleeding into minutes that feel like a thousand lifetimes before Gideon stands panting over Wendell, who lays pinned to the ground. Dark blood glints in the moonlight as it runs down Gideon's fur, a large gash trailing from temple to jaw. It drips onto the wolf laying on the ground, unable to catch his breath, a sickening grin splitting his bloodied face as his tongue lolls onto the ground. His beady eyes stare up at Gideon, filled with humor.

"*I knew she weakened you,*" he sneers, coughing up blood as it sprays over the ground. "*She's going to bring death to every one of us because all you wanted was a piece of ass—young and tight.*"

Gideon's paw crushes against Wendell's throat, and he brings his face down, staring into his eyes. "*You aren't worthy to share the air she breathes,*" he says, slow, calm.

Wendell's eyes widen just as Gideon's jaws clamp around his throat, a sickening crack echoing in the air.

The crowd erupts into cheers, hollering and yelling, clapping at Gideon's victory, but all I can hear is his last words repeating like a broken record from my nightmare—*she's going to bring death to every one of us…*

*LYCAN WITCH*

It feels surreal when the bar goes back to normal almost immediately after the fight. Occasionally, someone will come up and pat Gideon on the shoulder, congratulating him on his victory. Frank's smile is the one thing that's changed, not quite reaching his eyes as he serves everyone their drinks.

Gideon guides me into his office, ignoring the high of the crowd around us and shutting the door to drown out the noise. Peeling back the towels Frank wrapped around my hands, his jaw tenses. "I'm sorry," he says gruffly.

"It's... it's fine. It's my own fault for interfering..." I can't make eye contact with him, my gaze glued to the wounds. The ribbons of flesh on each side of my palms bleed, and my hands shakes, blood pooling and dripping down my fingertips.

Gideon gently lifts my chin, forcing me to meet his gaze, and it's all I can do to not stare at the quickly healing gash gracing the side of his face. "It's not your fault for wanting me to not be a monster," he whispers. "But, darling, you can't save a soul already bound to the underworld."

I wrench my chin free from his grasp, staring down at the floor. He sighs and begins cleaning my wounds. After he bandages the last bit, he sets my hands in my lap, getting up to walk to his desk and taking a swig of whiskey straight from the bottle.

"You heal fast, so it should be fine by the morning," he says, his voice flat and emotionless as he stares out the window. "I don't want you working here any more."

I want to argue. There's other things I could be saving up for now that Jules's tuition is covered, like paying Gideon back or getting a place of my own. But I can't find the words or the energy to defy him.

He turns from the window, finally facing me briefly before looking down into the bottle in his hands. "I'll have Frank drive you home."

The last sentence breaks my heart into a million pieces, as if he doesn't want me near him now that I openly showed his weakness to his pack. Now that I showed him I can't support the side of him that he needs to hold on to… the monster he needs to be to survive as alpha.

*The monster he needs to be to survive any attack from Monique. He can handle himself.*

I shake my wolf's voice out of my head, not wanting to hear her arguments. Tonight just shows we aren't good for each other. I make him soft—make him hesitate in a moment of battle, and tonight, I almost cost him his life. Wendell was right—the only thing I'm going to bring this pack is more death.

Standing from the chair, I walk out of his office without a word. I don't bother asking Frank for a ride home, the bang of the door closing behind me as I walk out into the night echoes through my soul. I bite the inside of my cheek as I avoid looking at the too-still wolf corpse lying on the ground and hear branches creak above me as Kaylus leaves his perch to fly down and settle on my shoulder.

"I don't want to talk about it," I whisper before he can say anything. I know he saw everything. I don't have an explanation for why I tried to stop Gideon, outside of my fear of him getting hurt, but there's also a part of me that didn't want to see him kill one of his own pack for me. Hushed voices drift over to me after I enter the tree line, and I slowly creep down the forest's edge toward it. Mumbling a spell under my breath and staying upwind of the noise, I do my best to mask my scent. My throat constricts when I remember the last time I used this spell—just a few weeks ago when I'd been sneaking into the Silver Lycans bar.

I shove the thought away as I get a clear view of a brown wolf, sneaking up to the office window. I don't recognize him as one from Gideon's pack, and though I haven't met all of them, the minute the wolf turns his head, his nose raised in the air for a moment, I know he isn't one of us.

Glowing golden eyes flit across the space, huffing as he turns back to the window.

"If you came here to—" Gideon says, his silhouette framed by the window.

*"I came here to warn you that if you don't make the right choice soon, we'll make it for you,"* the brown wolf says.

I don't understand why I can hear his voice in my head. After reading the werewolf books Gideon made me study, it should only be others in the pack that I can hear unless a wolf projects their voice to me specifically—outside of an alpha, who can hear any wolf's voice nearby.

The sound of glass shattering makes me jump, pulling me out of my shock. Shards of glass reflect the moonlight as they spray out of the open window at the brown wolf. Gideon launches himself outside, and the brown wolf laughs. *"Are you going to shift and fight me? That pretty pink wound on your face looks freshly healed, Disantollo. Did you win against some fat bastard by only a hair?"*

Gideon snarls, fur rippling over his skin. His jaw muscles tick, shoulders tensing, and his eyes narrow into slits.

*"Go ahead, shift! I've been itching for a reason to dethrone you."*

The wolf's words make Gideon still. "Get the hell out of here." He reaches up behind him to grasp the sill of the window, pulling himself up and inside. "And don't come back here, *Allen*, unless you're looking for your last fight."

The wolf laughs again, the sound making goosebumps rise along my arms. "*I hope she's worth it.*" He grins wickedly, backing away into the woods.

I hold my breath until he disappears, then move farther into the woods in the opposite direction, knowing exactly where I need to go.

## CHAPTER SIXTEEN
*Gideon*

YOU SHOULD'VE JUST KILLED HIM, MY WOLF SAYS, seething. He paces inside me, itching to shift and track Rathmann down.

Slumping onto my chair, I rub a hand over my forehead. "And then what? Kill the entire council when they come after us for retribution?" Looking out the window, I sigh, thinking of how Adara left.

*You're a ball of fuck ups,* my wolf growls.

"Damn it, I *know* that!" I slam my fist onto the desk, cracking the wood.

Adara called me a monster just weeks ago, and tonight, I proved her right. But what choice did I have? I knew that look on Wendell's face and how uncomfortable it was making her. His wandering fucking gaze is what landed him on my books the first time, when his wife caught him in bed with another woman—if she could even be called that. She was only seventeen.

I don't know how that sleazeball was able to convince her that she wanted to sleep with him, but I never stopped suspecting foul play—magic specifically. It isn't completely uncommon for a wolf to find a sympathetic witch, or even a witch so desperate for cash that she offers them an enchanted item. Sometimes it's to be stronger just before they challenge their alpha, but other times it's for things far worse.

I can't say I'm sad that he's gone. Anera begged me not to kill him, though I never understood why. They weren't mates, so it wouldn't harm her wolf.

Unable to sit in this office any longer with the scent of Adara lingering lightly in the room around me, I make my way into the bar, eager to see if Frank came back from dropping her off at home yet. Stepping through the door, I narrow my eyes as I see his auburn hair bobbing to the beat of the song Lucas's band plays. "You're back already?"

He looks up at me, one brow quirked. "Back from where?"

"Gods damn it all, did you drive Adara home?"

"No, was I—"

Shoving through the crowd of people, I stalk my way to the door, not caring about the rest of his sentence. Rathmann is out there, and if she's caught alone, there's no chance he'll let her get away.

*You shouldn't have let her go!*

"Shut up, you insufferable bastard!" I snap at my wolf. I shift, storming into the woods, but I can't pick up her scent.

My thoughts turn dark when I remember her mother coming into the bar, Rathmann lurking in the woods, Aramin showing up at the lake. All these threats, all these gods damn threats, and she's gone, untraceable, *again*.

I lope around the bar perimeter a few times, growling as I turn in the direction of my house, hoping she walked home and just wanted the time to think on her own.

*If that's what you think she did, you don't know her at all.*

Growling, I ignore him, despite knowing he's right. If I could find her scent somewhere between here and there, then at least I can follow it instead of calling out the hunter team again. Something I'd prefer not doing if I have the choice.

I'm just a few yards from the edge of my property, my hope of finding her or her scent dying out, when I hear the sound of wings beating against the night sky. Skidding to a stop, I lift my snout and sniff at the air, trying to find the raven I'm hoping is heading my way. It's only a second before I latch onto his scent, paws pounding on the forest floor as I chase after him. He caws as I barrel past him, swooping low to fly in front of me. He continues to fly, looking back once to caw again.

My heart pounds in my chest as I run behind him, wondering if Adara is hurt. Did Rathmann find her? Or her mother?

Holding back a growl, I push myself harder, faster, until I'm right up next to Kaylus, encouraging him to fly faster. I have to get to her—now.

The run feels as if it goes on for hours, and for a moment, I find myself wondering if he remembers where to go, frustrated that I can't ask him. When the scent I've been searching for finally hits me, I run past him. Adara sits on the ground, her knees pulled to her chest with her head bent forward, resting on top of them. Sitting with her back to a large oak tree, its branches creaking wearily in the breeze, bending as if reaching to comfort her.

*"Adara?"* I step toward her, unsure how she could get so lost in these woods when she has Kaylus.

Her head snaps up, gaze finding me, then narrowing as she glares into the branches. "I told you not to bring him here."

I stop, looking up into the branches to try to find the raven, but it's like trying to find the darkest part of a shadow in the night.

"I don't care if it's stupid!" she says. "Why don't you understand? It's the *only way*."

*"Hey..."* A twig cracks under my paw, regaining her attention.

"You need to go," she says, looking away.

Anger bubbles up inside me. *"Go? You're telling me to leave you here in the middle of the woods at night?"*

Her glare flicks to me. "I'm telling you to leave. I have to do this, and you can't be here, so just go!" Her hands ball tightly into fists, and silver dots her eyes.

"*No.*" I drop my ass onto the ground, sitting just a few feet from her.

Brows furrowed, she stares at me. "You don't even know where we are, do you?" She waves her hands around us. "This is Lockwood Forest."

I tilt my head at her. *"Why are you here?"* She isn't lost if she knows where she is. She obviously isn't hurt. *"Why didn't you let Frank take you home?"*

She scoffs, leaning her head back against the tree trunk and staring at the sky.

*"Are you that afraid of me?"*

Her eyes dart to mine, tears threatening to spill down her cheeks. "You're an idiot. The only reason I'm here is because I... because I... I can't watch you lose everything." She climbs to her feet, moving toward a break in the trees that seems to form a path, but it disappears into such darkness even my wolf sight can't pierce it.

I move around her, cutting her off and halting her. *"What are you talking about?"*

"I'm not worth this!" she says, throwing her hands up and gesturing between us. "I'm not worth you losing your pack or the council coming after you, or my coven. Gods, my mother wants to kill you—kill *us.*" She angrily swipes a stray tear from her cheek, her voice just above a whisper. "I'll get rid of my wolf, and it'll get rid of our bond. You won't be a target anymore."

Pain cuts through me like a thousand knives piercing my chest, and I barely register her walking around me as I stand there, glued to the ground like a fool. Kaylus caws, swooping just past my snout, breaking me from my nightmare.

I shift, sprinting to her and grabbing her wrist. I pull, spinning her into my chest, and my hand slides down, lacing her fingers with mine. She gasps as my other hand reaches up, cupping her cheek and brushing my thumb across her lips.

"Is that what you think will make me go away?" I ask, my eyes searching hers before watching my thumb drag over her mouth again. "I'll bite you a thousand times over until I prove to you where you belong." Dipping my head, I suck her bottom lip into my mouth and bite her, sweeping my tongue into her mouth as I kiss her, desperate to claim her mouth as mine —as desperate as I am to claim all of her over and over again.

She pulls away, the deep purple of her eyes swallowed by her wolf's silver, like two shining stars in this shadow-filled forest. "I'll get you killed, Gideon. Your whole pack. I—"

"Shut up."

Her eyes widen, and she opens her mouth to speak, so I press a finger to her lips.

"Shut up, Adara. Stop talking. Stop thinking." I slide my hand from her cheek until I'm gripping her neck and slip my other around her lower back. Pulling her to me, we turn until her back hits the trunk of a tree, and I press against her, pinning her to it. "I'm tired of repeating myself, so I want you to hear me now." My grip on her neck tightens as I bring her face to mine, my lips brushing against hers. "You will always be destined to be mine. By the fates, I will love you for eternity, your wolf be damned. Wish it away, keep it, it doesn't matter. You will always be mine." Closing the breath of space between us, I crush my lips to hers, willing her to hear me this time. To *feel* it—the truth of my words, the desire coursing through me, the love pouring out of my soul for her.

She kisses me back, desperate and clinging. Her nails drag down my bare back, and I move to trail kisses down her jaw to her neck, licking my way to her collarbone.

Then, I'm stumbling back as her two palms press against my chest and shove, and a growl tears from my throat.

"Gods, Gideon," she says, her voice trembling. She holds a hand to her mouth as she glowers at me. "You can't love someone you've known less than a month. Why are you so hellbent on being with me when all I'm doing is bringing danger into your life?" Shaking her head, she looks back at the path into the darkest part of the forest.

"Don't," I growl, stalking toward her.

Refocusing on me, her anger flares, seeping off her. "Don't what? Protect you? Is that such a horrible thing to do?"

"Don't pretend like you don't love me too." I step back into her space, forcing her back against the same tree as I hold her gaze. "Don't act like you're doing this for me when it's the most selfish thing you've ever done."

Her eyes flash, teeth piercing into her lip as her fangs come out. "What—"

"You want to protect me? *Fight.* Learn control, for gods' sake, but don't put this martyr shit on for me, darling."

She moves to shove me again, but I grab both of her wrists, keeping her hands on my chest.

"You want to get rid of your wolf so the bond disappears, but what if it doesn't? What if the bond stays and you just can't shift anymore?" Fear spikes in her eyes at my words. "There's no spell to get rid of it, Adara. Take some gods damn control of your life and make a choice. *Do something.*"

"I am!" she screams, pushing against me, but I don't budge. "I'm trying to get rid of all of this! My wolf, my fire, everything. I can't bear the thought of you dying because of me. If I get rid of this bond and my wolf, the council and my coven will leave you alone!" Tears stream down her cheeks, trailing through the smears of dirt. "If I get rid of my fire, my mother will leave me and Jules alone. It's the only way I can keep you all safe."

I press my forehead against hers, wishing I could erase the agony written on her face, the torment scarring her heart. "It isn't your responsibility to shield the whole world, Adara. Sometimes, you have to fight back."

Her face crumbles, and I release her wrists, wrapping her tightly in my arms as her body shakes.

"It's okay. It's okay, I've got you. You'll never fight alone, *mia fiamma*. I'm right here." I kiss the top of her head, smoothing a hand down her hair as she slowly gathers herself.

We don't say a word once she lifts her head from my chest. I stare into her eyes, wishing with every ounce of my soul that she would just accept her powers and fight for what she wants—all of it. Her wolf, her fire, her sister... *me.* Brushing a loose strand of hair behind her ear, I kiss her temple, my eyes closed, praying to the gods they'll let me keep her. I won't survive if they don't.

I step back to shift, and she copies me, shifting into the most beautiful black wolf I never want to go a day without seeing. Running alongside me, with Kaylus flying above us, we make the long way back home. But I can't shake the fear of the soul shattering heartbreak I'm worried is heading our way... unless I can remind her why being together is worth everything.

## CHAPTER SEVENTEEN
*Adara*

GIDEON KEEPS STEALING GLANCES AT ME AS WE run back toward his house, as if he's unsure whether I'll actually go with him or if I'll take off in a different direction at any moment. And maybe he's right. Maybe I would take off if I wasn't so exhausted from fighting against my instincts at every turn. The instinct that's begging me to stay close to him, that's screaming at me to stop running from him.

Even if that's the only way I know of to keep him safe.

*If you would stop being a stubborn fool, you'd realize you're safer together because that's when you're stronger.*

I glare at the ground, hating that I can't deny the truth in my wolf's words. The faint scent of palo santo swirls around me, and I freeze, sniffing at the air, trying to find the direction it's coming from. Gideon glances over at me as my head snaps in each direction. But I don't see any movement, and the smell of burned paper doesn't grow stronger in any specific direction. My eyes dart up to Kaylus, circling in the air above us.

*"Do you smell that?"* I ask him.

He widens his radius. *"No, and there's nothing moving in the woods. Why?"*

I scan the woods around us again. *"It's the dark witch, but it's faint."* Scowling, I strain my eyes through the shadows, but see nothing. *"Don't you smell that?"* I ask Gideon.

He tilts his head, then moves a few steps forward, using his paw to pin down a few low branches. The lake glistens behind him, reflecting the starry sky above. *"All I smell is the lake."*

I stare back at him, wondering if it's all in my head. We've been to this lake so many times. If the Lockwood witch is here, how have I never noticed before?

*"Swim with me,"* he says, nuzzling my snout with his.

The scent of the dark magic fades as the citrus, woodsy scent of Gideon fills my nostrils, making me think it really was just in my head. He turns away, bounding toward the water, shifting just before he breaks the surface. The briefest view of his beautiful naked form heats me up from the inside out, bringing back the memory of earlier today in the office. Warmth pools low inside me, and my mouth goes dry. His head pops above the surface, shaking wet curls out of his face as he smirks at me, beckoning me to him with one finger.

My wolf lurches me forward, throwing me into the water before I can think twice. I shift, gasping as the cold lake touches my bare skin, and Gideon laughs beside me. He wraps one arm around my waist as I try to splash him, touching his nose to mine. "Good girl," he whispers, his breath hot against my mouth.

My thighs ache at those words, and I wrap my arms around his neck, pressing my lips to his. His arm tightens around me, lifting me, and my legs come up to circle his waist, crossing my ankles at his back. My body seals to his, my hands burying into his hair, tugging him closer.

He spins, kicking his legs as he floats on his back, his mouth never leaving mine as we near the shore. The minute we get into shallower water, he flips us over, my back on the sand and the waves lapping at my hair.

My hands roam his body, clinging to him, desperate to have him fill the aching void in my chest. I moan when he slips a hand between us, his finger circling my clit before diving inside me. My back arches as he curls his finger inside me, tiny fireworks exploding behind my eyes.

He bends down, his breath hot against my ear. "Come for me, little witch," he whispers before bending down to capture my nipple in his mouth, sucking and biting. His finger doesn't slow its assault, driving into me.

I can't catch my breath, my chest heaving as my toes curl, and my hips coming up to meet his every movement. "Gideon," I whimper, wanting more, needing more of him. "I want you."

He lifts his head, looking down at me. His dark wet curls falling across his face, dripping water onto my chest. Tears threaten to pour down my face as I stare into his eyes—eyes filled with desire, with lust, with... love. The mate bond in my chest throbs, the pain making me gasp worse than the first time.

*Accept it. You need him*, my wolf says softly.

"I-I need you," I rasp, the words barely audible over the lapping water around us and our panting breaths.

A slow smile breaks across his face, and I moan when he pulls his finger from me, the cold water splashing up to meet my hot center.

I suck my lip into my mouth, biting down on it, and gasp when I feel the tip of his cock at my entrance. He rubs it against my clit, and I tilt my hips, wanting him inside me and needing more friction at the same time.

His deep chuckle vibrates against me as he presses his bare chest to mine, one hand lifting my chin, the other gripping my hip. "Gods, you are gorgeous." He presses his lips to mine, slowly rubbing his tip against my clit again. "Incredible." Another kiss. "Perfection." He sucks my lip into his mouth, his tongue sweeping across it, making me moan. "Mine," he growls, pulling back to position himself at my entrance and thrusting inside me, filling me in one quick motion.

I cry out, lifting my legs to wrap around his hips. His fingers dig into my side, pulling me to meet each thrust as he slams into me. He kisses along my jaw, trailing slowly to my mouth, as his hips slowly pump into me. When his lips finally find mine, my fingers tangle into his hair, and my tongue darts into his mouth, stroking his tongue. The need building between my thighs is desperate, fierce. My thighs tighten around his waist, and my hands pull him harder against me, crushing his lips to mine so hard my fang pierces into my lip.

"Adara," he moans, his voice husky.

I've never liked my full name, always reminding me of Monique, but gods, if I don't love the sound of it falling from his lips right now. "Please, Gideon."

"Please what?" he says, kissing my neck, the whisper of his words on my wet skin making me tremble.

"Make me come." I close my eyes, tilting my head back to allow him better access as a growl rips from his mouth.

Picking up speed, he slams into me. Harder. Faster. His teeth graze my neck, then his tongue before he bites me, hard. I scream, pleasure bursting inside me as I ride the building wave. When his thumb finds my throbbing clit, I rasp out his name, which only seems to fuel him.

My nails drag down his back, pulling on his hips, wanting him deeper still. Then, the wave crests, and my pleasure peaks. My body arches, lifting to meet him, and I come so hard I see stars. He curses in my ear as he comes inside me. The spill of warmth fills me, and I open my eyes, taking in the star filled sky above me.

Gideon rests on top of me, bracing himself on his elbows as his fingers twirl in my hair. "I love you," he whispers.

My eyes snap to his, but he isn't even looking at me. He's watching as a wet strand of my hair is wound around his finger.

"I love you beyond any doubt in your mind, beyond the moon above us. I love you as infinitely as stars in the sky." His hand moves to cup my face, finally bringing his eyes to mine. Storm clouds framed by wet curls, the color of shadows. "I will fight anything and anyone to keep you by my side, including you. I would follow you into the depths of Hell without a second thought. I love you, Adara. I won't let you push me away."

Tears fill my eyes, blurring my vision, and I reach up to brush my fingers across his cheek, thankful his face is healed and not scarred from earlier. My heart swells, knowing he only wants to protect me, and I can't deny the fact that keeping him safe is all I want too. "I love you too, Gideon."

"Promise me you'll stay." He searches my face, wiping away the falling tears racing down my temples.

"I promise." At that, the cord tying us together vibrates for just a second before it relaxes, lifting a weight from my chest. A sigh escapes me. "I promise I'm not going anywhere."

He kisses me, softly at first, then hungrily. I kiss him back with every ounce of love I can muster, letting go of every worry I've been holding on to. His cock moves, still buried inside me, and this time, it's slow and passionate, filled with whispered *I love you*s, soft touches, and gentleness. The moon and stars the only witnesses as we give into each other, baring our souls as we tattoo the other onto our hearts for a lifetime. For eternity.

---

It's nearly sunrise by the time we get home. I bury myself under the covers after taking a shower, curling onto my side as I check the communicator. A smile stretches across my face when I see a message from Jules, gushing over the academy and her roommate.

*She's so cool, Addy. It's Wren's first year here too, and we get to start together. We even get to explore campus for the last half of this semester and just hang out.*

I laugh, picturing her excitedly dancing around her dorm. *Maybe I'll come visit soon and meet her.*

*Really?!* she sends back. *Can you... do that?*

For once, I'm grateful for Monique. Because of her, Jules knows I'm a wolf and why I can't stay with her at Chloe's, though she doesn't know exactly where I am now. The less she knows, the better. The safer she is.

*I'll look into it, okay? Now go be happy and have fun.*

*Are you happy? Safe?*

I stare at her message for a while, chewing on my lower lip. Happiness feels weird... unfamiliar, but I have to admit, weird feels good. Gideon's face flashes in my mind, and my cheeks flame, my lips stretching into a smile. *Yeah, I am. Love you, Julesy.*

*Love you, Addy.*

"What're you smiling at?" Gideon climbs into bed behind me, crawling over to mold his body to mine, his chest against my back. He presses featherlight kisses to my ear, trailing down my jaw.

"Nothing," I say, smiling as I turn my face toward him, gently kissing his lips. Snuggling down into the covers and his embrace, I close my eyes, ready for sleep to take me.

*"Addy?"* Kaylus says, ruffling his feathers as he burrows down into his nest sitting in the open window.

I peek at him, staring into his black eyes.

*"Stop looking for the well. You've survived this long with practically no magic. Now you're strong enough to fight*

*back.*" He turns his head around, nuzzling his beak under his wing. *"We don't have to just survive anymore."*

Tears pool in my eyes, one dripping over the bridge of my nose and across my cheek, soaking into the pillowcase. *"No, we don't,"* I whisper back silently, unsure if he hears me as sleep relaxes his body.

The warmth of Gideon's body seeps into me, and the weight of his arm presses me into the mattress. Soon, sleep easily pulls me under.

---

A low rumbling pulls me from the first dreamless sleep I've had in a while. Grumbling, I roll onto my back and shove Gideon's shoulder. He sighs, reaching onto the side table and snatching his phone. He squints at the screen, the sunlight slanting through the window and across his face. His light gray eyes are rimmed in dark stormy gunmetal, and I brush the hair off his forehead with my fingers. He tosses his phone back onto the table after typing a message, smiling as he turns onto his stomach, burying his face in my hair. I laugh when I hear him sniff, pushing at his shoulder.

"You smell delightful, have I told you that?" he mumbles, sleep still evident in his voice. He groans when his phone vibrates again, small bursts over and over. "What?" he snaps, answering the call as he lays on his back, lacing his fingers with mine. "When?" He presses his lips into a firm line. "Fine." He sighs, tossing aside the phone once more.

"What is it?" I ask, lifting onto my elbow as I look down at him.

"I have to go. Council meeting." He cups my cheek, brushing a thumb over my lips.

I shiver at his touch, chills snaking down my spine and pooling between my legs. "Another meeting?"

"I don't want to go, either, but I need to." He lifts up, kissing my lips before getting out of bed. "Frank will be here soon. He'll stay here with you while I'm gone."

My mouth pulls down into a frown, worry settling heavy in my gut. "I don't like this, Gideon. I want him to go with *you*. You can't go by yourself."

He runs a hand through his hair after tugging on his slacks. "I'll be fine. I don't want to leave you here alone."

"So, call Mila. Or Madrona. Or Darrold. Don't go there by yourself. I... I don't trust them." I chew on my lower lip, my wolf pacing nervously inside me.

Opening the closet door, he pulls a white button-up off the hanger and slips his arms inside, slowly buttoning it together. "I'm not asking you to trust them. I'm asking you to trust me." He looks at me from beneath his lashes, thick and black, like the wavy hair falling across his face.

I crawl over to where he sits down on the bed to put his shoes on, wrapping my arms around his chest and laying my head on his shoulder. "Promise me you'll be okay."

His chuckle rumbles in his chest, vibrating against my ear, and he reaches around to pull me onto his lap. "For you, I promise I will be more than okay." He kisses me, sweeping his tongue across my lips, then growls as the doorbell rings.

"Here! In case anyone needs a, uh, heads up!" Frank calls up the stairs, chuckling as his footsteps fade into the house.

"I'll see you in a few hours, little witch." He nips at my bottom lip gently before getting up to cross the room.

I watch from the bed until he disappears down the hall, stepping down the stairs, and I listen for the front door to shut behind him. The sound of the lock clicking into place makes tears prick at my eyes. The memory of the maniacal expression on the brown wolf's face from last night makes me take a shaky breath, and I bite the inside of my cheek, looking at Kaylus.

"*I'll watch him.*" He caws once before flying out the open window, soothing my frayed nerves slightly.

## CHAPTER EIGHTEEN
*Gideon*

I TUG ON THE COLLAR OF MY SHIRT, HATING THE formality of these godsforsaken meetings. I push down on the pedal of my truck, choosing to drive instead of shifting to run so I don't have to get dressed in this suffocating outfit twice. I drove by Aaron's house, then his garage before making my way toward Vermont. I don't know exactly what the worm is up to, but I haven't heard any more rumors about him challenging me for alpha since the night Aramin came to the lake, and both his usual spots were quiet. The road stretches out before me, and a scowl crests across my face. Between those two and this meeting, something isn't right. Grant refusing to move the meeting outside the lodge just added to the suspicion crawling through me.

*"We want to discuss the issues within in your pack that have been brought to our attention. There's been an exile and a death in less than a month, Disantollo. It's pack standard to have a meeting immediately for these circumstances,"* Grant said.

I shift in the driver's seat. It is pack standard, but...

*But it's suspicious.*

"Exactly," I mutter, agreeing with my wolf. It's why I had Frank stay behind with Adara.

It's a few hours before I reach the dirt road to the lodge, and by then, my teeth begin to ache from the force of me clenching my jaw. After the warning note outside my office window and Rathmann's follow up visit, I have no doubt that this is a set up, but whether it's my life or Adara's they're after, I'm not sure. I'm confident I can handle myself, though, and knowing Frank is there to protect Adara gives me some peace of mind.

My skin tingles, my wolf itching to come out. I park, straightening my shirt as I step from the truck, and walk into the lodge. The air feels stale here, unsettling when the wind should be blowing and wildlife should be scuttling around the forest. I pass through the large glass doors, nodding at the receptionist sitting at the front desk as I make my way across the polished wood floors to the elevator. Shoving my hand into my pocket, impatience wears my nerves thin, and I storm from the doors before they fully open.

I don't bother waiting to be called into the meeting, shoving the oversized doors open and gathering the attention of the entire council as their heads snap up to me. "Councilmen, good to see you're all here on time."

Grant folds his hands on the table. "We were. You, however, are fifteen minutes late."

I smirk, lounging back on the chair left for me. "I didn't have much notice. Couldn't be helped."

I lazily look around the table, noting that Rathmann is especially calm today. My wolf paces at the observation.

"What's on the agenda, boys?" I ask. "I have a bar to run, so I'm afraid this meeting will need to be more of a chat."

Grant sets his jaw, staring hard at me for a moment before speaking. "There's been a few complaints recently that we need to discuss. First, Wendell..." he glances down at the paper before him, "Clark."

Sighing, I cast my gaze out the window, taking in the view of the forest. "What about him? Can't really cast a complaint if he's dead."

"His death is the complaint, Disantollo," Grant says, slapping the table. "Why would you kill your own pack member?"

I look pointedly at his hand, slowly bringing my gaze to his weathered face. "Because he wasn't worth keeping alive."

"The report says he *looked* at that witch, and you killed him for it." His eyebrows shoot to his hairline, lips pressed into a firm line. "Is that all it takes now? Just looking at her?"

"You didn't seem to care much about him before, like when he lost all rights to his house or when he cheated on his wife with a *child*—"

"She was seventeen—"

My eyes cut to Rathmann, quieting him immediately. "I never released that detail in my report."

He puts his hands up, smirking. "Heard it through the grapevine."

My gaze narrows at him, suspicions from earlier swirling through my head before looking back to Grant. "Wendell died because he attacked me. As alpha, any attack on me is an immediate, undisputed challenge, and he lost. Not sure where you're getting your information from but—"

"And what about Aramin Hayward?" Grant says, leaning back in his chair. "Did she also challenge you?"

"She's none of your concern," I say slowly.

Grant raises his brows. "Isn't she? A packless, feral she-wolf turned away from her own pack for what? Doing her duty as a wolf and informing us of a bitten witch? Sounds more like she deserved a promotion in your ranks."

A dry laugh escapes me. "Being a snitch and a gossip doesn't mean you're raised within the pack ranks. And being unable to follow orders or have any gods damn common sense means I have no room in my pack—at all. Not for that kind of weak minded bullshit."

He slowly nods his head. "I see. So, this witch—that you've stated is your mate—is the root cause of you exiling one she-wolf and killing another wolf. All within a month's time."

"Is there a question in there?" I ask, sighing. "Is there any point to this insufferable formality? I run my pack as I always have—without you." Standing, I tug down my sleeves, adjusting the buttons. "I'll be going—"

"Going? So soon?"

My heart drops at the sound of the voice, and I whirl around. Blonde curls frame emerald eyes, and the stench of her sickly sweet perfume makes me gag. "How the hell did you get in here?" My nails lengthen into claws, readying to shift and attack.

Monique laughs, the trill sound piercing.

I don't miss the flinch of each councilman at the table, nor do I overlook their lack of surprise at seeing a witch in the lodge. I glare at them, keeping the woman in my peripheral. "What the hell is going on?"

Rathmann's eyes light up. "Monique has been *so* helpful. She's been able to tell us exactly where your stupid little hybrid is and how to capture her. Can't be too hard with her lack of magic, right?" A sickening smile cracks his face in half, and I fight back the urge to tear it off him. "Apparently, your *girlfriend* is wanted by her own coven for treason. Isn't that something?"

Grant holds up a hand, silencing Rathmann's laughter. "Monique, we were told you'd deal with this...

issue of the bitten witch. We'll handle Disantollo ourselves."

"Of course," she says, smiling from Grant to me. "You were so much fun to play with, Gideon." The way her lips form my name is wrong, making my skin crawl. "Though, it was such a disappointment that you were able to fight my curse charms so well."

Glancing between the council and Monique, the pieces slowly click into place. The stale air around the package outside my window, just as stale as the air outside the lodge today. The fog clouding my head, changing my wolf's voice, making me distrust Adara, and the way she mentioned it so casually at my bar.

"Think of all the suffering you could've avoided if you would've just rejected her from the start. But no." Her eyes narrow into slits. "You had to *fall in love*. You had to *accept your mate bond*. You had to *protect* her and ruin my curse charm at every turn." All the rage melts from her face as her smile comes back, making my stomach turn. "Ah, but all the fun I'll have with her now."

The doors burst open behind Monique, the red head of my nightmares swaying over the threshold. A tight leather dress, as red as her hair, hugs Aramin's curves, her heels clicking over the hardwood floors. She brushes past Monique without a glance, heading straight toward Rathmann. "You called." She stops right before him, popping one hip out as she purses her lips.

"I called three hours ago," he hisses. "Sit down or get out. You're interrupting the council."

A small flash of anger sparks across Aramin's eyes, but she looks at Grant with an apologetic look. "My apologies, sir." She bobs her head once before moving to stand at the back wall. She catches sight of me, claws out, and huffs a laugh.

"I don't have time for this," I growl, shaking my head as I move toward the doors to leave, but Monique sidesteps into my path.

"Make time then," she says, her lip curled in disgust.

I keep walking, invading her space until my face is inches from hers. "I should've killed you the minute she showed up on my doorstep. Bleeding. Covered in *soot*." I sweep my gaze down her body, traveling back up to her narrowed eyes. "If not then, I should've killed you when you went to lay your hand on her again in my bar. Move before I decide that this is the perfect place for your life to end—among the very creatures that you hate." Anger boils inside me, and my fangs grow, piercing into my lip. I want to kill her now, but the need to be with Adara and protect her from whatever plans Monique has set into motion overpower that bloodthirst growing inside me.

Monique grits her teeth, nostrils flaring. "I don't take orders from half-bred fleabags. Back up before I *help you*."

I shove past her, not wanting to waste my time any more than I already have, but just as I reach the door, a bolt of lightning spikes through me. I crumble to the floor with a shout, wrapping both arms around my stomach as nausea roils through me.

Heels click behind me before the bottom of Monique's stiletto presses against my throat. She quirks a brow at me lying on the floor, but I can't move. My body is rigid, my muscles stiff and unyielding, and my wolf is stuck inside me.

I can't shift.

And I can't move.

And I can't hear my wolf.

A lazy smile spreads across her face, and she presses down harder with her heel, the sharp end piercing into my throat. "What's the matter," she whispers, mirth dancing in her eyes. "Witch got your tongue?"

## CHAPTER NINETEEN
*Adara*

"YOU SURE YOU DON'T WANT TO TRAIN?" FRANK asks, peering over at me from the kitchen doorway.

I shake my head, giving him a small smile. "I just want to relax today." I turn back to the TV, hung high up on the wall in front of the couch. One of my favorite movies is on, one I used to watch with Jules when Monique worked late, and the nostalgia is crippling. I miss my sister.

Thinking of Jules leads back to Gideon—the reason she's able to enjoy her time at the academy—and I find my gaze trailing back to the front door. My wolf snarls at the foreboding fog surrounding us, pushing me to conserve my energy and not waste it on training. When I came downstairs, I begged Frank to follow Gideon to the meeting, but he refused. I'm the alpha's mate, not the alpha, and though he'd never say something like that to my face, the difference in power is undeniable and frustrating, like pleading for a hundred year old tree to move when you refuse to carry an ax.

He didn't even take his cell phone with him, leaving it where he'd tossed it onto the nightstand by the bed. I sigh and try to focus back on the movie, one of those mindless romantic comedies where you know the plot and the ending within the first ten minutes, but it doesn't make you enjoy it any less. At this point, the guy is rushing around trying to find the perfect cake for his current, toxic girlfriend, then stumbles into the bakery owned by a beautiful woman, who you know will steal his heart.

Dragging myself into the kitchen, my stomach grumbles at the smell of food and coffee. Frank stands at the counter, bacon sizzling on the stovetop as he cuts up slices of tomato. He lifts his head, pausing to look at me with a smile. "Hey, help yourself." He points with the end of the knife at the coffee pot. "Fresh pot. This'll be done in just a minute. You like BLTs, right?"

He smirks when I nod, gratefully pouring myself a mug of coffee. With the stress like lead in my stomach, I haven't had an appetite so far today. "Thanks," I say, bringing the mug to my lips and inhaling the sweet scent of caffeine and sugar.

He bobs his head a few times. "Yeah, yeah, of course. Can't let you waste away on my watch."

The coffee is quick to sour in my stomach as I look out the window and check the branches—bare and empty with no Kaylus in sight. Sighing, I slide onto a stool, staring into my half-full mug.

"He'll be fine, love," Frank says without looking up. "It's not the first time Gideon's had the world against him."

My mouth pulls down into a frown. "It's the first time it's been my fault, and he went by himself, Frank. *Alone*. He's only one man. How..." I blow out a breath, staring up at the ceiling as I try not to cry.

He sets the knife down, coming around the island to pull me into his arms. "It isn't your fault. Your mother and whatever she's doing is her doing and hers alone. You can't take responsibility for that. It'll only ruin you inside." He pulls back, holding on to my shoulders as he looks in my eyes, his reminding me of warm chocolate on a winter's day—full of the promise of comfort. "He's one *alpha*, not just a man. He's been alive for centuries with the council starving at his back, waiting for the perfect moment to drive their knife into him. He won't let it be today." The corners of his mouth lift slightly, then he presses a kiss to the top of my head before bringing the plates to the island. "Now, eat."

By the time I'm choking down the second half of my sandwich, the bacon doing wonders for my nauseated, empty stomach, gravel is crunching under tires out front. I ditch the remainder of my sandwich on the plate, falling off the stool in my rush to the front door. Frank chuckles behind me, but I don't care—I need to lay eyes on Gideon and make sure he's alright.

Grabbing the doorknob, my throat tightens and my stomach curdles, the aching in my chest so painful I bite my inner cheek. I squeeze my eyes shut and throw open the door, releasing the breath I'd been holding as I watch Gideon step down from the cab of his truck. He looks over at me, his black hair falling in front of his eyes briefly before he brushes it to the side.

The burning in his gaze steals my breath—pure hatred rolling off him in waves. The lunch and coffee I just ate lurches to my lips, and I fight to keep it down. My wolf panics in my chest, begging me to move out of the way as he crosses the front yard and climbs the steps to the door. I can't breathe, my lungs won't expand and air won't enter. He's never looked at me like this before, not even when he caught me cheating in his bar, and I struggle to believe it's real. When his hand shoots out in front of him, grabbing the front of my shirt, the shock feels like a brick on my heart.

He drags me down the hall, throwing me into Frank as he shoots off the stool, catching me before I hit the ground. "Get her the hell out of my house!" he yells.

I bury my face into Frank's shirt, unable to watch whatever nightmare this is as it unfolds before me. My arms tremble as I latch onto his forearm, and my legs barely hold me up. Footsteps approach from behind me, and Frank turns slightly, shielding me from Gideon.

"Did I stutter?" Gideon asks, his voice low and dark, slowly enunciating each word. "Do you need me to repeat myself? Get. Her. Out."

"I..." Frank shifts, glancing between me and Gideon. "Why? I thought..."

"You thought?" Gideon's cologne surrounds me as he leans closer, making tears prick at my eyes. It smells off, but I can't place it as he screams beside me. "Thinking isn't your job! Here, I'll show you."

I whimper as he fists the back of my hair, my nail digging into Frank's forearm. His other hand reaches out, grabbing Gideon's wrist. "Stop it," he growls. "This isn't you. What's going on?"

I chance a look at Gideon, immediately wishing I hadn't. His lips curl up into a hideous smile as he stares down at Frank's hand holding on to his wrist as he clutches my hair tightly, pulling strands from my scalp.

Gideon's other hand flashes by my face, gripping Frank's throat. He laughs—maniacal and unhinged—as Frank grapples against his fingers, trying to loosen his grip. "Is this more like me? Should I kill you for touching her?"

"G-Gideon, stop," I say, struggling to get the words out around the lump in my throat. "Stop this. Please."

His laughter grows, and he pulls me back against him, tugging my hair to make me look up at him. "This whole time I've hoped that your powers would grow, but instead, you're still just as pathetic as you always have been. Powerless, helpless, begging others to do things for you. Make me stop, Adara," he threatens, his gray eyes darkening like the clouds of a hurricane. "Or do you not care about his life?"

He releases my hair as he throws me to the ground. I land on my hands and knees, smashing my forehead on the floor. I reach up to grip the countertop, struggling to my feet as I scramble away from him. Frank's face is turning red, and his panicked eyes stare back at me, pleading. "If this is some sick game for training, Gideon, stop!" I wish he'd let Frank go, apologize, make some twisted excuse at trying to awaken my powers, like the last time he pissed me off just to make me lose control.

But this is worse. Worse still when he shakes his head in disgust.

"You think this is a game?" He tilts his head. "You think I'm *joking*?" He looks back at Frank, releasing his throat, but my breath of relief is sucked back in when Gideon rears back and punches Frank in the nose. Blood gushes down his face, and he lands hard on his knees.

"No!" I scream, rushing forward and reaching for Frank, but Gideon snatches my hair again, ripping me off the floor. My feet hover over in the air for a moment, then he throws me down the hall.

*Run*, my wolf says. *Run!*

My heart shatters right there in the hallway, staring up at the man I gave myself over to as he stalks toward me. I trip over my own feet as I push myself over the threshold of the front door, tears streaming down my face. My eyes frantically search the yard, the forest, everything—trying to figure out what to do as reality hits me.

I can't use my fire on him—my heart just won't let me.

I close my eyes for a brief moment, trying to tap into the mate bond and access his strength and speed, just as I did in the lake before, but the bond won't open. "No, no," I mutter, the hollowness in my chest growing.

My wolf can't outrun his without that power.

I can't win.

He launches himself out of the door, his shoe stomping onto my back and shoving me to the ground face first. I squeeze my eyes shut, willing it to not be real. This is a nightmare. It has to be. Gods damn it, why can't I wake up?

"Still here?" he teases, whispering in my ear. "It's almost like you want me to hurt you." He stands, and his foot slams into my ribs. I scream, feeling the bones crack, and curl into the fetal position as I try to shield myself. "Is this what you want, Adara? To be treated as the traitor that you are?"

*Get up!* my wolf snarls. *Fight back, you fool!*

My palms heat, but the minute I open my eyes, the flames die under my skin. Gideon's face swims in my vision, blurred by the tears.

"You're pathetic," he spits, bending to reach for me again, but I fling myself to the side, away from him.

My legs shake as I get to my feet, my wolf pacing inside my chest, confused and wary. I won't win against him in a fight—he could shift and tear me apart in wolf form or beat me senseless in our current form, proven by the throbbing spot at the back of my head and my various broken ribs.

Slowly backing up, I shove my wolf deeper inside me, refusing to allow her to come out when we can't tap into the bond. The world tilts and spins before me, but I force myself to keep my eyes on Gideon as I move farther back. Dark amusement flashes across his face, a wolf enjoying the chase as he plays with his prey.

He throws his arms wide. "The monster you always thought I was, right?"

Blood coats my tongue as I bite hard into my cheek.

He chuckles. "You thought I loved you." He takes a slow step forward, and my heart rate quickens, knowing he could reach me in a second, but his words—

"I love *you*," I whisper, hoping it'll break him from whatever hell he's crawled from. "I love you, Gideon, and whatever this is, you have to fight through it!"

"You think this is a spell?" he says, incredulous, before dissolving into another chuckle. "This isn't a spell. This is me, darling. This is me!"

I brace myself for his body to slam into mine, for his hand to grab my throat or my hair, for another fierce blow to my already broken ribs, but a car flies down the driveway, gravel spraying in every direction as it swerves around Gideon's truck and spins around.

"Get in the car, girl!" Mila yells, fear and anger warring on her face as she looks behind me at Gideon.

I throw myself at the car, clinging to the door as I hear him snarl behind me. I'm barely in the seat before she hits the gas, and I have to pull hard to slam the door shut, narrowly avoiding Gideon's truck bed. "F-Frank—" I stammer, turning around in the seat to look at the house fading in the rear windshield.

"Who do you think called me?" she says, pedal pressed to the floor as she flings the car onto the two lane road and peels down the pavement. She takes a quick glance over at me, her lips forming a thin line. "Girl, you shouldn't even be asking about him. You're a gods damn mess." Her eyes dart to the rearview mirror. "For good reason. Gods, by the fates, I swear today is just wickedly bad."

I try to force myself to relax back against the seat, but my muscles tremble, and as the adrenaline fades, the pain becomes unbearable. I suck my bottom lip into my mouth and bite down, whimpering at the searing pain in my side.

Mila glances over at me, frowning. "I got you. I know exactly where we're going, okay? Just hold on for a minute longer."

I squeeze my eyes shut, willing us to move even faster to wherever we're heading and praying to any god that can hear me that they'll have something to help this pain. But really, if the gods are listening, they'll hear the true prayer beneath that—one for the man who broke my ribs as he became the monster of my nightmares, one for this pain in my heart that splinters my soul.

Save him, save him, save him.

Because if they can save him, then maybe they'll save me too.

## CHAPTER TWENTY
*Gideon*

"ADARA!" I ROAR, STRUGGLING AGAINST THE enchanted chains binding my wrists to the cement floor. I fling my body at the glowing ball floating in the space just outside of my reach. "Adara!" My chest heaving, I glare at the witch's device, sweat trailing down my back. I reach down inside me, trying to pull my wolf to the surface, but I can't even hear his voice. And for once, I miss the insufferable bastard.

A chasm opens in my chest as I watch the projection within the ball. Frank tries to stop me, but only suffers for it as I grab his throat, holding on to Adara's hair. Fear is written across her face, and I beg the fates to stop this.

"Adara!" I yell once more, falling to my knees as she's tackled to the ground, my foot striking her ribs—hard. I know that blow broke her ribs, but she still refuses to fight back. "Do something! Fight back!" I try to tear the chains out of the floor again, but the bolts hold firm, the metal clasps around my wrists biting hard into my skin. Hot blood trickles down my hands, dripping onto the floor off my fingers.

But I can't rip my eyes off the scene playing out before me. Monique stalks toward Adara in my body, and bile rises up in my throat.

"I love *you*," Adara whispers, pain filling her voice. Her hair hangs in a mess around her shoulders, and her shirt is smeared with blood. Tears track clean lines down her face, and her voice shakes as it gets louder. "I love you, Gideon, and whatever this is, you have to fight through it!"

"I love you too," I say softly, wanting to carve my heart out and hand it to her so she'll never again mistake another for me.

But I can't blame her for believing what's standing right before her eyes because the way Monique looks, the way she talks, is so close it's damn near perfect. The nicknames, the temper, the violence... Gods, after fingering her way through my mind, Monique was able to grasp a few small memories, and it was just enough to make her act believable.

Monique chuckles at Adara as she backs away, and my gut tightens, unable to stop watching my worst nightmare come to life. I wish I'd listened to her before I left this morning. Maybe if I'd brought Frank with me, it wouldn't be like this. Maybe—

But maybes and regrets won't fix anything.

A scream rips from my lips, scratching my throat, burning my chest. My heart is on fire, and my soul cracks as the mate bond between us frays.

I can't lose someone else to these witches. I can't lose her.

A small white sedan flies down the driveway, whipping around my truck and spewing gravel in every direction. Mila sits behind the steering wheel, and I've never felt such an overwhelming amount of relief, of gratitude. I clench my jaw as a lump forms in my throat, watching Adara throw herself into the car as it tears back down the drive toward the road.

Rage paints itself on my own face staring back at me through the magic ball, and laughter bubbles out of me. The irony of Adara getting away from Monique with the help of the wolves she tried so hard to teach her to hate isn't lost on me. Tears stream down my face as I lay on the cement floor of the lodge's basement, staring up at the ceiling, unable to tame the wild laughter pouring from me.

Monique's hatred of my pack will only grow after this—after Adara ran to me for help the last time Monique attacked her, and now another one of my pack has helped her escape for a second time. The small bubble of joy I felt at the reflected rage the crystal ball showed me is quick to burst—because Adara doesn't know that it wasn't me.

That it wasn't me that hurt her. That looked at her with hatred and disgust. That thinks she's pathetic and powerless. Because I *know* she isn't. She has more power than any witch I've ever met, including her hellish mother. A small, sad smile spreads across my face—once Adara learns control and can grapple with the full extent of her powers, wolf and witch alike, they'll all suffer. They'll burn at her feet when she discovers the torment they've caused.

---

A faint clicking pulls me out of a sleep I must've slipped into. Looking around myself, I see a sliver of moonlight pouring from one of the high up half-windows at the top of the basement's walls.

Sighing, I roll onto my side, my wrists throbbing fiercely. I pull them to my face, looking over the deep gashes in my skin, unable to heal while these cuffs stay on me and suppress my wolf and his powers. Monique's spell shouldn't be able to last indefinitely, and when it wears off, I can only hope that my pack won't be in shambles and Frank will still trust me.

I close my eyes, wanting to go back to sleep and into the dream where Adara lays wrapped in my arms, when I never go to the lodge and choose to stay with her instead. Or the dream before that where we weren't werewolves at all, only humans, living ignorantly, blissfully unaware of the supernatural world around us.

My head snaps around as a loud screech sounds by the window. A shadow moves past the glass, and I squint into the dark night, trying to make out the movements when the glass shatters. I pull my hands over my head, shielding myself from the shards raining down above me. One pokes into my hand, and I freeze when it happens again and again. Lowering my arms, I find myself face to face with two beady black eyes. The raven tilts his head from side to side, ruffling his wings, his feathers glinting in the low light of the moon.

I blink a few times, not believing that this bird—this familiar—is really sitting before me. He hops away, moving to the window, and I struggle into a sitting position, the chains clanking together with the movement. "I can't..." I let my words trail off as a wolf slips through the window, struggling through the small opening before falling inside and landing on its paws.

It shakes out its auburn fur, moving toward me, and chestnut eyes meet mine.

"Frank?" I say, my voice hoarse as I try to hold back tears. I shake my head after a minute, raising my wrists. "Enchanted chains. I can't hear you. I can't even hear my own bastard's voice."

He walks over to me, inspecting the chains before padding back to the window and looking outside. A bundle falls through the open frame, heavy as it thuds against the cement floor. Frank shifts, his body unfolding as he stands to his full height. He bends down, unfurling the wrapping and lifting a set of metal bolt cutters. He throws me a smile as he lifts them up. "Came prepared, boss."

I shake my head again. "They're enchanted." Glancing at the window, I clench my jaws at the worry piercing through me. "You shouldn't stay long, Frank. If—"

He raises a brow. "You worried about some council pricks suddenly? Or the bitch who punched me while wearing your face?" He bends down, clamping the cutters around one of the chains encasing my wrists. "The Gideon I know wouldn't let a witch beat his mate the way she did and get away with it. He sure as hell wouldn't be telling me to leave his ass in some dungeon in the woods while his mate suffered out there, thinking it was really him who hurt her." He grunts as he snaps the cutters, the metal falling away, then raises his eyes to mine. "I told you I came prepared—with enchanted bolt cutters. Give me some credit."

He makes quick work of the second chain, and I rub my sore wrists as the metal falls onto the ground. My wolf's powers surge through me, his strength giving life back to my tired muscles.

*You gods damn fool*, he growls.

I chuckle under my breath. "Missed you too, you mangy bastard." Glancing up, I watch Kaylus fly in circles above my head before looking back at Frank, who tosses the cutters up through the window. "How did you know?"

Frank looks at me over his shoulder, his gaze flitting to the raven. "A little birdie told us."

I narrow my gaze at him. "Kaylus can't talk to anyone but Adara."

He laughs, mirth dancing in his eyes. "Still can't take a joke. The raven came to us after getting some… unexpected help. A coven witch."

"A witch?"

He gestures out the window, ignoring my question. "Come on, see for yourself."

I move toward him as he shifts and jumps through the window. I let my claws lengthen, staring down at my hands, the wounds on my wrists already healing. The raven glides down, landing on my shoulder, and presses his beak to my cheek. I shrug him off, and he flies through the window after Frank's mahogany wolf. "Idiots," I whisper, a smile gracing my lips briefly before I shift and jump through the small frame after them, curious to discover the witch who's decided to help me.

The relief that pours through me as my suit is shredded when I shift is unmatched, like a breath of air after being buried alive. I'm not sure what I expected when I jumped through the window, but it wasn't a young woman with light brown hair and bags under eyes. Glancing around the gathered group, I recognize everyone but her. Darrold's blond wolf stands beside her, Kaylus circling the air above us.

Frank stands before me, now shifted back to his human form. "Gideon, this is Chloe."

A small smile spread over her face. "Hi," she says softly.

I shift, narrowing my gaze at her. "Explain."

She flinches at my voice, but nods. "I cast a familiar spell, which lets me talk with another witch's familiar, like Kaylus." She gestures above us to the raven, who caws. "He told me everything. Apparently, Addy asked him to follow you here, so he came to get me to help. After the familiar spell, he brought me to... um..." She looks over at Darrold.

"Darrold's house," Frank supplies.

"Yes. Sorry," Chloe says sheepishly, struggling to make eye contact with me. "I was able to tell him what happened, and he brought me to Frank. I enchanted the bolt cutters while they regrouped and went over whatever details." She lifts one shoulder in a shrug. "Now, we're here."

"Why would you help me?" I ask, looking around the forest, waiting for a trap.

Chloe huffs a laugh, humorless and sad. "I have more in common with Adara than you'd realize. I've been trying to update her on Monique's plans, but once she shut down our office, I lost my job and all my access." She wipes a tear from her cheek. "It's my fault. I should've worked harder, attended council meetings. I should've grown my powers to be able to join the huntresses or something. I—" Covering her face with her hands, she takes a shaky breath.

Darrold steps closer to her, nudging her elbow with his snout.

Sniffling, Chloe wipes her cheeks with the heels of her hands and looks at me. "I know Adara, and I know she's happy with you. She's meant to be a part of your pack. I won't let Monique take that away from her if I can stop it."

I take her in, from the bags under her eyes to the guilt weighing heavily on her shoulders, making them slump forward, as if she's curling into herself. Glancing up at Kaylus, I heave a sigh. If there's anyone I trust to have Adara's best interests in mind, it's the raven. So, if he's the one who got Chloe for help, then I trust that he knows what he was doing.

Looking back at the three faces before me, I nod. "Alright. Let's get back, then figure out what's next."

## CHAPTER TWENTY-ONE
*Adara*

WITH A SIGH, I ROLL OVER IN BED AND STARE AT the peach colored wall. The sun rises, the first rays of light peeking in through the window behind me, and I watch as the light makes shadows dance across the wall. It's been three days since I came to stay here with Mila. Three days since my mother showed up, using a charm to look and sound like Gideon. I inhale sharply through my nose, my anger rising at how easily she was able to trick me. I should've known it wasn't him—and a part of me did, looking back on it. I knew he smelled off, but it didn't hit me until later that it was because his cedarwood and caramel scent was mixed with patchouli.

I throw the covers off with a huff, sitting up and cradling my head in my hands. I let her run me off. I let her beat me down, breaking three of my ribs along with Frank's nose. And what did I do in return?

Nothing.

I did absolutely nothing.

The only thing I still don't understand is why she's always alone. Why is she not with the huntresses? Why are they not with her when she comes for me?

Knowing about the curse charm, and remembering her coming to the bar, it just doesn't add up. None of it makes any sense.

Why wait to take me down on your own when you could come with an entire team and be successful?

Unless...

Unless she wants to harness my immortality for herself.

Unless she's working alone for a reason.

Thinking that makes my stomach sour, but it's hard to deny the truth of it all, the likelihood of it happening. Not only do I have fire magic, that she's tired to suppress my entire life, but now I'm an alpha's mate. It's like dangling a fresh, bloody steak before a lion's den. Monique can't resist the temptation of gaining immortality, but also all my power.

"Addy?"

The sound of Kaylus's voice makes me jump, and I snap my head around to look at the window where he sits, perched on the sill.

"Are you okay?"

I shake my head. "No," I whisper. "I'm not." I fling myself back, laying on the pillows and pulling the blanket up to my chin. "I let her win, Kaylus. How will Gideon ever be able to look at me the same again?"

He tried to come by after being released from the council's dungeon—a dungeon, for gods' sake. Chloe and Mila crowded around me, explaining everything that had happened at the council's lodge, with Monique there, and how she was able to be so... convincingly Gideon-like. But I couldn't bear to face him.

"I let him down. I showed him exactly what he feared I was from the beginning—weak." Turning my head to the side, I look at Kaylus, his sleek black feathers bright orange in the bright sunlight. My face crumples as sobs steal my breath.

*"Addy... Gideon loves you for who you are, not how powerful your magic is."* He hops over the sill and glides onto my bed, nuzzling his beak into my hair.

"How can I stand beside him like this, Kaylus? I'm not strong enough to be an alpha's mate. I-I can't control any of it."

*We can't stay away from him forever until you decide you feel worthy enough*, my wolf says, aggravated. *You need to get over yourself. You're the only one that thinks you're weak.*

"What if you could get stronger?" Kaylus asks.

"What?" I whisper, snapping my head toward him.

He sighs. *"I hate suggesting it, but... Lockwood's witch, in the clearing, she had embers in the air. Almost as if she could use—"*

"Fire magic," I finish, sitting up.

*"Exactly,"* Kaylus says, nodding.

"Instead of wishing away my powers, I could wish to get stronger. To get more control."

My wolf perks at the idea. *And I can train you as we hunt for her.*

A small smile breaks across my face, hope dancing in my heart.

A knock sounds on the door. "Addy?" Mila calls through the wood.

I smooth a hand down my hair, getting up to open it. "Hey."

She smiles tentatively. "There's someone here to see you."

My eyes dart to the stairs behind her, my heart rate quickening.

"No, it's not him." She shrugs when I look back to her, reaching out to touch my arm. "Come on." Pulling me by the hand, she guides me down the stairs and into the living room.

Her house is cozy—an oversized couch with plush blankets on nearly every seat. High carpet that feels like walking on clouds is spread throughout the house, and each wall is a calming pastel type of color. It's easy to feel at home here, and as I come into the living room, I see a familiar face.

"Addy!" Jaz rushes from her spot on the couch, launching herself at me.

I catch her in my arms, stumbling back a couple of steps as she buries her face in my shirt.

"Gods, I thought you were hurt. I-I thought..."

"Shh," I say, brushing my hand down her hair and squeezing her tight. "I'm alright. It's alright."

She pulls back, misery written all over her face. "No, it's not. Gideon... he... he's broken."

My brows furrow at her words, and I glance up to find Madrona on the couch, Chloe seated beside her. "Broken?"

Madrona glances between me and the girl clinging to my arms. "He's... sad, I imagine. Losing the main source of light in your life will do that to a person, especially the second time around."

I bite the inside of my cheek, remembering his family that my ancestors murdered.

"We just came to check on you, dear," Madrona continues, smiling over at Mila and Chloe, then Cali as she bounces in from the kitchen. "I see you have quite the group of friends here for you as well."

"Yeah," I say, guiding Jaz to the other side of the couch and sitting down with her. "They've been... life-savers, really."

"Mm, I could imagine." A gleam shines in her eyes. "Well, we didn't want to take up much of your time. We should get on our way. But it would do well to remember, love." She comes over, brushing my hair back from my face with all the kindness of a mother, bringing tears to my eyes. "All the light in the world can only be appreciated in the dark, just as hope is most valued during times of despair." Reaching down, she grabs Jaz's hands with a knowing smile.

"Thank you," I say.

"Of course, dear," she says before walking out the door.

Chloe comes over and grabs my hand, and we spend the rest of the day sitting on the couch with Mila watching sappy romcoms, trying to ignore the weight of the real world as it closes in around us.

Just as she has for the last three days, my wolf drags me to the window the minute the sun sinks behind the trees, desperate to lay eyes on Gideon. Unable to fight her, I crawl through the frame onto the lower roof below, shifting and jumping to the ground. I take off into the woods, following the tug of the mate bond in my chest. I swallow past the lump in my throat as I near Frank's house. A soft glow comes from his windows, and I wait, pacing within the tree line, until I see him.

Gideon runs a hand through his dark hair as he makes his way over to the couch. The pallor of his face makes the last crumbling bits of my heart shatter like shards of ice, and it takes every bit of strength within me to fight the urge to go to him. To wrap him in my arms and apologize for every bit of pain he's endured because of me.

Closing my eyes, I sigh, my breath coming out as a misty puff in the cold autumn night air. Soon, I'll go to him. But I have to get stronger first. Monique is still out there—same as the council, same as my coven. I have to get stronger.

So strong I won't have to choose between my wolf and my magic. So strong that I'll keep everything I love—both Gideon and Jules. My pack and my witch heritage.

Steeling my nerves, I take a deep breath and turn away from the house, from Gideon, disappearing deeper into the woods, toward Lockwood Forest.

I'll be damned if that witch sends me away tonight, because right now, I have nothing to lose... and everything to gain.

## CHAPTER TWENTY-TWO
*Gideon*

THE HOLD IN MY CHEST HAS ONLY GROWN larger.

I fling myself down onto Frank's brown leather couch, unable to stomach being in my own house after what happened. I'm tempted to set the whole place on fire, but I can't bring myself to even go down the driveway right now. Staring up the white ceiling, I try to block out the voices drifting over from the kitchen.

"He can't just mope around here," Madrona says.

"You weren't there. You didn't see him... or her." Mila's voice shakes, and the expression of terror written on her face when she went to rescue Adara flashes through my mind.

Frank sighs. "You're both right, okay? He can't mope forever, but the man deserves some time to think—"

"Three days is plenty of time," Madrona snaps. "Kilch is still—"

"Adara still won't talk to him?" he asks.

"No," Mila says, "and I already explained it all. Chloe even came over and talked to her, but... she needs some time."

Growling, I shove myself up from the couch, stomping through the living room and slamming the front door behind me. I climb into my truck, grateful Frank was able to bring it over from the house, and drive.

I avoid the bar and the lake—both filled with too many memories of Adara—and just drive around town. I roll the windows down, resting my arm on the door. The breeze is cold, but I welcome it as it numbs my fingers.

I tried to go to Mila's when we got back, unable to keep myself from checking on Adara, but the way she refused to see me was enough to ruin every hope of a happy ever after. Now, Mila and Chloe have both tried to talk to her, but she's...

Well, I don't know what she is. She won't talk to anyone, and she won't see me at all.

My knuckles turn white as I clutch the steering wheel.

My wolf has been quiet, and I can't help but wonder if it's just another curse charm, suppressing more of my power. After they threw those chains on me, Monique told me about the first one she'd tried—the curse charm that made me distrust Adara and want to distance myself from her. It explained the fog clouding my mind when she first came to stay with me after. Unfortunately for Monique, our mate bond made that charm nearly impossible to maintain.

Turning the truck onto a dirt road, I find myself parked in the middle of a trail. Fields of asters, pansies, and chrysanthemums spread out to each side of me, deer wading through the tall grass in the far distance. I watch them graze, wishing I could be as mindless as the simple beasts before me.

*You'd have to learn to follow orders to be mindless.*

I scoff. "Impeccable timing. I was just learning to love the quiet." I keep my eyes trained on the wildlife at the far end of the field, mildly relieved to hear my wolf.

*Stop moping around like some useless low ranking wolf and get your shit together.*

"Don't—"

*I was the one trapped in that godsforsaken prison when you got yourself chained to the floor. Now I'm telling you I won't allow you to make the same mistake twice. You want your mate back? Go claim her.*

Anger surges through me, and I punch the steering wheel. "I can't!" I yell, spooking the deer who lift their heads, then dart from the meadow. "She's won't even see me because—"

*Because you let that witch hurt her* again, *so fix it*, he growls. *Fix it so you can reclaim your place as alpha with her by your side. Or are you going to let the council, Monique, and soon Kilch ruin everything?*

Growling, I slam the gear shift into drive and peel down the dirt road, heading back into town. My tires squeal as I peel into Aaron's garage parking lot and slam on the brakes. Rage courses through me, and I welcome the rush of it, the familiarity of the anger making my blood heat and pound through my veins.

Three cars sit in front of the shop, and I stalk past them, ripping the door open as I step inside. Keith's buzzed blond head snaps up from where he'd been bent over some paperwork, his jaw going slack and his eyes wide.

"Where is he?" I ask, leaning back against the wall.

"Uh... who?" Keith asks, the tremble in his voice betraying the lie.

"The one who wants to be the new alpha. Come on, Keith, you're smarter than that." One side of my mouth lifts into a lopsided grin. "Then again, you weren't smart enough to save Adara from your stupid drummer before he got himself into trouble, were you?"

He licks his lips, his eyes darting to a door off to the side with tinted glass.

"Perfect." I push off the wall, heading straight for that door, ignoring Keith's sounds of protest from behind me. Throwing it open, the door crashes into the wall, and the smell of cigarettes hits me like a train. My lips curl up in disgust, my eyes adjusting to the dim light in the office. The blinds over the one window in the back are shut, and the overhead light is off. A small lamp sitting on a desk covered with scattered paperwork gives off a dim yellow haze.

"What the hell?" Aaron says, jumping up from his chair behind the desk.

"Ready for round two?" I hold my arms out to each side. "I'll let you get the first hit, drummer boy."

"W-what?" His eyes dart over my shoulder, finding Keith and, I'm sure, the panicked look covering his face.

"Isn't that what you've been bragging about? All the hits you'd get on me in an alpha challenge? How much you've been dying to fight me to take over the pack?" I storm into the room with large strides, and Aaron backs up from the desk, stumbling into the blinds covering the window.

"I-I never wanted to fight you, boss," he stutters.

"Didn't you?" I narrow my gaze at him, slamming my palms on the desk. "That's what I've been told you've been spewing around town with your fucking mouth."

"N-no, I swear!" He holds up his hands. "Aramin wanted me to challenge you, but I-I told her she was crazy. I didn't want to sign my own death warrant, y'know? She got pissed and took off. I haven't seen her in a-a few days or some shit."

My vision tunnels. "What did you say?"

"I didn't challenge you. I like actually being alive."

Aramin. Of course it was Aramin and her fucking bullshit. Images flash in my mind—her sitting on Aaron's lap every shift she worked, dragging him into the bar on the nights he didn't even have a set to play, how she always draped herself all over him and his wannabe-alpha-asshole personality. A snarl rips from my mouth, and I throw all the papers off his desk, launching the small lamp at the wall. The bulb on it shatters, and I stalk from the office, stomping back to my truck.

I drive myself to Anera's shop, my truck parked in one of the Main Street spots. Staring in the window, I realize her shop is open. With Wendell's death, I assumed she'd have shut down the sandwich place, letting herself mourn in the upstairs apartment. I realize how wrong I was when I see her standing behind the sandwich counter, laughing at something her customer said before waving goodbye. The customer walks out of the shop, and Anera turns around, singing along to the radio as she dances behind the counter, cleaning as she reorganizes her ingredients.

My legs feel like lead as I pull open the door, the small bell jingling overhead and announcing my arrival. Anera looks up, and she smooths a hand over her frizzy brown hair, various curls escaping her bun. I give her a small smile. "Hi, Anera."

She lets out a rush of air and smiles. "Gideon." Her eyes fill with tears as she rounds the counter toward me, wrapping her arms around me. "I'm sorry I haven't been by since... the other day. We were all told to give you space." She pulls back to search my face, her brows furrowing. "What's happened?"

"I..." My voice cracks, and I clear my throat. "Did you file a complaint with the council over Wendell's death?"

"Did..." A loud laugh bursts from her. "Gods, no. He was a piece of scum, dear. He deserved it after all he's done." She pulls me into the shop, pushing me into a chair at a table and rushing back behind the counter.

I stare after her, confused. "Someone filed a complaint with the council, Anera."

Setting a plate with a triple decker club sandwich down before me, she slides into the opposite chair. Her lips press into a firm line. "It wasn't me."

"But you'd asked me not to kill him before." I rub a hand over my face, my stomach grumbling at the scent of the sandwich wafting up at me.

"I did," she nods. "But that was years ago, Gideon." A darkness shadows her face briefly before she takes a deep breath. "That girl he slept with was just a child, but she was old enough to know what she wanted. I never believed him, though. Always suspected magic, but I couldn't prove it. I didn't want you to kill him then, but only because I wanted to get to the witch who gave him such a power."

"Did you?" I raise a brow at her, but she shakes her head.

"No, I didn't. I only ever got a name and a description of what she looked like. But spells can be cast to change appearances, and names can be fake." She shrugs, looking out the window at the street outside. "I can give you what information I gathered, but I'm not sure it'll be much help."

Nodding slowly, I lower my gaze to the plate before me and pick up the sandwich, taking a bite. Maple turkey, honey ham, and applewood bacon mix together with muenster cheese, herb mayonnaise, and spiced mustard. The lettuce crunches with each bite, and the tomatoes are sweet and juicy. My mouth salivates as I swallow the first bite, diving into the next immediately. With everything happening, my appetite has been nonexistent. Until now.

Anera smiles, reaching out to pat my arm. "Good, yeah? You come by here for lunch every day. I don't want to hear a thing about it."

"Thank you." I finish the sandwich, downing the bottle of water she brought for me. I close my eyes, replaying Kilch's words in my head. "Did something happen in the last few days, Anera? Something with Aramin."

Her brows cinch, but she nods slowly. "Actually, yes. She came by a few days ago, giving condolences for my loss." She scoffs, rolling her eyes. "As if that sprite would ever actually care about someone else's loss."

I clench my jaw for a moment, trying to control the anger building in my chest. "What did she say, exactly?"

She sighs, scrunching her mouth to the side. "Let me think. Something about she was sorry for my loss. That she was sure I was so upset and angry. I laughed in her face, told her it was the best thing to ever happen to me. I have all our money and a successful business and now no moochin' husband to support." She shakes her head. "I should've left him ages ago and given up on ever getting information on that stupid witch." She lifts her gaze to mine. "She did say something else, though. She patted my hand when she got to the register, saying something about how she'll get justice for my pain, but when she touched me... it hurt."

"Hurt?" I look down at her hand, inspecting the spot where her fingers rub.

"Yeah," she whispers. "Like a bad shock."

*Magic*, my wolf snarls.

I shove back from the table, placing my hand on her shoulder. "Thank you. I'll be back for lunch tomorrow. Please report to Frank if Aramin comes back here."

She frowns up at me, confusion evident in her face, but she nods.

I get back into my truck, flying down the road toward my bar. Loathing consumes me as I think of Monique—showing up at my bar, abusing Adara her whole life. Now, joining with my kind—the wolves she hates—just to ruin the speck of happiness Adara had finally found.

A dark laugh escapes me with one thought: we do have one thing in common. I hate my kind too.

The council will pay for the pain they've caused, and Monique's punishment will be without comparison—worse than anything from her nastiest nightmare.

Everyone needs to be reminded of why they fear the wrath of Gideon Disantollo, the Silver Wolf Pack alpha, and Adara needs to be reminded of everything that we are because I refuse to live in a world where I never get to see her smile, never get to kiss her lips. Where she never feels true happiness again. Where she doesn't believe how powerful she really is, my little lycan witch.

Thank you so much for reading the second part of Adara and Gideon's story.

Please consider leaving a review on Goodreads or Amazon. Every review helps bring more visibility for new books.

Keep reading for a name guide and the blurb for book three, CAPTIVE WITCH, coming winter of 2024!

# NAMES: PRONUNCIATIONS AND WHAT THEY MEAN

Adara Morrow: a-dah-rah moor-oh – flames of tomorrow
Juliana: joo-lee-ah-nuh – youthful
Monique: moh-neek – alone

Gideon Disantollo: gid-ee-uhn dee-san-toh-loh – great destroyer, Hades
Ella: el-luh – fairy maiden
Grace: gr-ay-s – blessing

Frank: fr-ay-nk – free man
Mila: mee-luh – friendly
Aramin: ar-ah-min – mint (based on Minthe)
Darrold: dar-oh-ld – pride and honor
Kurtis: kur-tiss – refined
Lucas: loo-cas – bringer of light
Vera: vair-uh – faith
Cali: cah-lee – lovely
Brent Poltan: ber-en-t p-oh-l-than – hill, one who belongs to regiment

Allen Rathmann: ah-len rah-th-man – great counselor
Raymond Grant: ray-muh-nd gur-an-t – protecting, tall

Madrona: mah-dr-oh-nuh – mother goddess
Jazelle: jah-zeh-l – pledge
Bella: bell-luh – beautiful

Wendell: wen-del – wanderer
Anera: ah-neh-ra – sand

Keith: kee-th – woods
Aaron Kilch: ayr-ren k-ill-ch – strong fish (codfish – *Peter Pan* inspired)

Chloe: k-loh-ee – servant of Demeter
Batya: bah-tee-yuh – heavenly
Celeste: sell-leh-st – daughter of god

Sawyer: soy-yer – woodcutter
Tristan: trih-st-an – sad

# THE STORY CONTINUES...

Don't miss the breathtaking sequel, CAPTIVE WITCH, coming this winter 2024!

**One mistake threatens my fall—the bitten witch captured by a hunter.**

Everyone knows not to cross Gideon Disantollo, the dangerous alpha of the Silver Wolf Pack, and every witch knows not to enter his territory... But after I'm bitten and changed, I discover that Gideon is my mate—and the reason my powers are spiraling out of control.

But when the wolf council and my mother join forces, I realize how screwed we are—and how desperate I am to keep Gideon safe.

Now, I'm clinging to the last bit of hope that I can find the well and grow these powers that I never wanted in the first place... while trying to convince my wolf that staying far away from our mate is the right choice—for now.

Because Gideon and I are stronger together. After all, I am the alpha's lycan witch mate...

Find it on Amazon!

Story updates, ARC reader opportunities, and fun freebie extras available when joining the monthly newsletter! Visit www.whitneymorsillo.com to join.

# ABOUT THE AUTHOR

Whitney Morsillo is a New England transplant living in the Tennessee mountains and writes paranormal romance. She has a master's in creative writing and believes books are crucial to survival in this wild world because "whether life is good or shit-tastic, you deserve an escape to beautiful men and to run with the wind in your fur... or hair." When she isn't writing swoon worthy, morally grey men who find their sassy fated mates to be their greatest strength—and infuriating weakness—or beautiful villains with tragic pasts, she looks forward to the changing leaves of autumn, drinks way too much Earl Grey tea, and reads her children *Harry Potter* while sneaking in some steamy reads after bedtime.

Follow her on [Facebook](), [Instagram](), [TikTok](), and [Amazon]()!